LOVEDON

MARION CRICK

LOVEDON
LOVE DONE?
LOVE IN LONDON?
LOVED ON?
YOU DECIDE...

ODE TO ROMANCE

Writing of love can be as difficult as finding love.
It flits all ways, with delight, being cruel, emotions erupt,
It lands, and it leaves, hovers, flutters like a dove.
The realisation can be slow, evolve, or thunderbolt abrupt.

The souls involved each have a different approach,
The path of true love is not a set route.
Different types can find love together, without reproach,
But some fall apart, their paths in dispute.

Love is not about sex, lustful advances or carnal desire,
It's far more complicated than that, as our lovers discover.
Search your world for those you know, attract and admire,
Your answer may not be obvious, but a result to uncover.

LOVEDON CHAPTERS

Lovedon/ Second Edition

By Marion Crick
Published by CCLLP at Lightning Source LLC
Copyright 2019 M Crick

This book contains adult content from the start.
Please do not continue if you would find this offensive.

ISBN 978-0-9573125-7-9

July 2013 / Second Edition March 2019

This is a fictional story.

Some of the names, titles, sequencing, areas and dates in this book have been amended to ensure that this work portrays a fictitious experience rather than those of any other individuals or companies.

Any similarity is purely coincidental. This book is also an expression of the personal opinion of the author.

Pick one at random
The new book by Marion Crick
ISBN 978-0-9928281-6-5
February 2019

ACKNOWLEDGEMENTS

Marion Crick would like to thank her family, friends and past and present acquaintances for their help and support in creating the tapestry that is her life and the source of many of the tales within this text. Without this rich variance of situations that they have provided, her work would not be as diverse as it is.

Thank you for the experiences of the good, the bad, the difficult, the love, loving, companionship and wealth of observations you have all provided in your own ways.

Also to the people Marion never met, just observed from a distance. They have added colourful and valuable fabric to the mix that has been weaved together.

Lovedon

THE SUMMER OF 2012 *AND* LONDON *WAS* BUZZING!

I. COOLING HIS EMOTIONS

The steam poured from the white-tiled double shower unit, water spraying at full pelt on to the broad shoulders and head of Giles as he refreshed himself from the heated day in his London office; frustrated by both his work and his intensifying desire for Kathy, the new Communications and Social Media Manager at his national advertising company.

His strong pale torso had not enjoyed the benefit of a suntan over the last eighteen months, as he prefered to throw himself into his work to try and avoid the mental pain of the breakup of his previous marriage; the warmth of sunshine holidays a distant but nevertheless fond memory. The zesty lemon shower gel lathered easily over his defined shoulders as his slowly rotating hands moved to his broad chest. He had a small but very obvious Captain Caveman tattoo cartoon character at the top of his right arm, which he regretted from the day after the night before it painfully arrived. Giles's advancing years and his elevation to owner of the company made this regret grow; he hoped that its cheeky gaze would fade, but to no avail. His cleansing ritual continued downwards, past his navel to his maintained waistline and on to his blond pubic hair and over his ample manhood. From his early years onwards, he had known for many years that he was proudly not lacking in this department. He rolled his fingers firmly and purposefully around his phallus and a gentle and suggestive tingle shot to the tip of his water-soaked, warm manhood, before he manoeuvred further between his legs to ensure that no area remained unwashed. His wet hand's enquiring journey continued over his firm defined thighs and, with his sturdy back arched, still further to his tight, muscular calves to complete his cleanse. His tactile investigation continued and the day's covering dissolved with the water that danced against his smooth skin and travelled down his body to the chrome plug hole on the white, shower base to his size ten feet. He stood for an extra moment below the gushing flow of the showers face turned upwards directly into its travel to absorb its energy on his face before catching his breath as he withdrew, turning the jets to silent and stepping out of the cubicle to towel his body down. Steam filled the bathroom and he felt a release from the day by the experience, although the memory of Kathy remained firmly imprinted at the forefront of his mind. He reached for the folded white towel to dry himself, before applying a little lotion to his face and exited to the main bedroom.

In trying to keep trim, for himself rather than for any possible future admirers, Giles endeavoured to keep fit and stop his waist line from expanding further. He would occasionally take to cycling energetically around the lanes of London, preferring his own bike to the somewhat popular and therefore not always available, sponsored blue cycles, referred to as 'Boris bikes', dotted around various locations to his office. However, he did not like the 'MAMIL' title (middle aged man in Lycra) that subsequently followed from anyone who knew him, and, more importantly, the regular incursions into his path by buses and lorries. Also, the weather had been so poor that cycling into work dry did not mean that you came home without getting soaked. He could think of more pleasant experiences of getting wet. Living in the 'Green and Pleasant Land', as the hymn goes, usually required rain, but that summer, the summer of the London Games, proved to be exceptional in providing so much precipitation.

Having an eye for detail, as would be expected from an advertising executive, he liked to be smart in his appearance and invariably dressed in a work suit, but drew the line at wearing a tie. He preferred the 'very smart, but approachable' look to the plain 'accountant' wrapper many of his contacts sported.   If the summer weather allowed, his choice changed to dark pressed Bermuda business shorts. Giles liked to see himself as 'of the time', but other colleagues mocked his style openly, in a good-humoured way.

He had been a high flyer in the city; the hustle and bustle of London life and the advertising world suited him in his younger days, however, somehow he knew that the high pressure may not be doing him any physical favours as he spotted ever deepening age lines. A younger man's game, he prided himself on staying ahead of the change curve when it came to promotion and advertising, and had made it to the top, but not without personal marital cost.

Giles had rented an apartment in the old sand-brick and pollution-scarred buildings of St. Katharine Docks. He had been there for just over a year, but was looking for a more modest and affordable accommodation to the south or east of London. He didn't really mind the cost of his current, long-term unaffordable, residence though because it was summer. The city was beautiful and the London Games had really brought a previously unknown buzz and welcome distraction to his newly found, although initially unwanted, freedom following his acrimonious divorce, which was starting to be consigned to his memory banks.

Giles was conscious of his age, knowing that the years were not going to reduce from the thirty-eight already attained. He was 5ft 8in tall, slim build and starting to struggle to keep it all 'hanging north'; his blond thinning curly hair tried to remain youthful, with the previously mentioned annoying and regrettable small shoulder cartoon tattoo from one forgettable weekend in his twenties. His spectacles arrived in his mid-twenties, giving him an air of authority, aided by a slowly receding hairline. His divorce was completed about eighteen months earlier and, after some transition, he was looking for new love to fill the void left by his cheating wife of seven years. She was long gone. She lived in a 'des-res' in leafy Wimbledon with half his cash and pension, and had a baby with her old boss, a child that she had never wanted with him.

She stayed in contact occasionally, but only usually because she had forgotten something important and needed a memory jog. He usually accommodated such requests, as long as his work schedule allowed.

He had, however, kept the cat, Duster, a middle-aged Persian house cat, also a Tom, who, although neutered (Giles was convinced that the cat never forgave him for that), now kept him company most evenings as he found that he was getting a little too old for the wild social life he used to enjoy pre-marriage. When he says he kept the cat, his ex-wife took the cat, and then returned it to him when she found out she was four months pregnant, suggesting that Duster had missed him. How convenient! That was nearly two years ago and best left alone now.

His company's office was convenient to his apartment, close to Monument, and was not far to travel by foot or by pedal, subject to the weather. He also had the option of the bus, an alternative he resisted to maintain his fitness if he could. The office was clean, modern and dynamic in style, his chosen preferences, and based in an older building which had its issues from time to time: mainly boiling in the summer and freezing in the winter. The high, dark blue screen divisions in the large, open-plan office were not conducive to a full view of all who participated in the company's success. Instead, they created individual project areas to avoid contamination and replication in advertising programmes, and only provided glimpses of the usual incumbents and any new joiners or contractors who added to the mix. Giles had found himself seeking out a view of Kathy, or an opportunity to say good morning. She had joined in the spring of the same year and was becoming a pleasant and an ever-growing distraction to his daily routine. Sure, they had chatted at the water dispenser and joined the crowd at drinks after work, but he had not been able to really introduce himself as the Giles he wanted her to know. He was slightly regretting his decision to introduce the 'cube farm' style office furniture system three years earlier to stop such fraternisation, clearly now understanding the objections he received at the time. He had partly argued at the time that this was to stop any Cupid's arrows flying around the office, but it seemed to be him that had been struck.

Kathy had also completed the fall-out stage of her divorce; re-negotiating and re-establishing emotional boundaries with all those involved. This had taken her a couple of years to achieve and had taken some emotional soul searching and resolve to succeed. She was a young at heart forty-one year old; Jess, her daughter, now aged seven, saw to that with all the running around and child social diary juggling, an art in itself, that she usually required. Kathy was thankful for this because she did want to restart her life again. The divorce not being the end, just a new beginning. She had always been attentive to her appearance, and this was clear from the depth of her confident beauty. Her well-groomed mid-length auburn hair was silky in appearance and regularly cut. She had mascaraed brown bright eyes, and manicured painted nails. She would often try to jog in the summer around her village and go to the gym when the weather closed in, to keep her 5ft 6in petite frame in check. The commute and walk around London also helped to keep her figure looking good. Her new managerial role was demanding, as she liked it, so she wanted to be as fit in mind as she was in body and the team she managed kept her on her toes. She occasionally succumbed to the odd cigarette or two to calm the nerves where required and to relax in the evening after the commute home to Kent.

For Kathy, her divorce had been a gradual dying of an initially loving relationship, rather than an explosive, 'you should have thought about this before you slept with . . .' type end. Both parties valued different opportunities as they matured and arose. They had married at a young age, Kathy in her early twenties, enjoying some early life halcyon days, deciding later on to have a child which, on reflection, may have been a way of holding the union together for longer than it should ,as it fizzled out. With their maturity, and for the sake of their daughter, they had kept conflict to a minimum to release each other from their marriage. Matt, her ex-husband, and relocated north with work some twenty months earlier, soon after their separation, and the divorce decrees were granted at a distance, with no party overly contesting their marriage's demise. An agreed, trumped up unreasonable behaviour charge against Matt was cited to get the divorce through. The reality was that they both just wanted to head in different emotional, physical and geographical directions. With Matt wanting to move north and Kathy wanting to stay close to her parents and Kent, the final straw was broken.

Her unflustered, understated strength and beauty radiated wherever Giles saw her. Magnetised by her radiance, her well-spoken calming voice, and her toned physique, his admiration of Kathy was tangible. His distraction was becoming obvious to both him and to a few of his colleagues. His desire to get to know her grew each time he met or saw her, noticing something new, distracting and even more beguiling each time.

2. SO MUCH SAID IN A TWEET

The need for Giles to get to know Kathy had not subsided since he met her on her first day some three months earlier. He was becoming aware that she too had noticed him in their brief office encounters during their day-to-day bustling working lives. Giles was not a shy man; he would not have got so far in business by being so, and was finding this personal hurdle for some reason a tall order. He had dated a few women since his divorce, but this had never really amounting to anything, other than a bit of fun and the occasional energetic, usually alcohol fuelled, frolic.

In their separate ways, both Kathy and Giles had investigated internet dating websites, with varying and disappointing results. The TV and magazine ads that they had individually observed both in a professional and personal capacity were of interest, and each had decided their preferences. With most contacted respondents over-describing their attributes (the reality mainly being very different in their individual experiences), it was obvious that sometimes these 'suitors' were only looking for no-strings attached sexual encounter or some form of tainted love, rather than a relationship of any real meaning.

It was the word 'meaning' that meant everything to Giles, wanting to reach personal fulfilment in a relationship, rather than physical desire, although he was a man and had needs in this direction.

Their work paths crossed on a semi-regular basis, attending the same meeting occasionally or having a group discussion about a particular issue, either in its own right or as part of a bigger project. To maintain team morale, Giles arranged an occasional trip to the local bar for drinks and dinner for anyone who wanted to hang behind after work. Giles made the most of these opportunities to chat with Kathy, freely admitting to himself afterwards that his approach had usually been clumsy for this or that reason. He knew that she mattered to him, and above all this message was getting through to Kathy who was enchanted by his enquiring efforts, although, she chose not to let on. With its long warm evenings, the summer was more conducive to these types of outing, which were billed as a team building benefit. With project group colleagues intermingling, his opportunity to really have any meaningful time with Kathy, to find out about the woman he desired, were limited, usually with Kathy leaving early to get her train home to Kent. In these short encounters, his mind fizzed as he consumed her persona and his desire to be with her was not extinguished, but only fuelled further.

Giles had realised that he now had a fear of rejection when starting to re-engage with new people in a relationship format, fed up with the very occasional and energetic, but hollow, one night stands, and what he described un-affectionately as 'gold diggers'.

He knew that Kathy had noticed him, but was strangely confused as to how to go about an appropriate approach he wanted to be remembered for. As pioneers of all forms of communication, many office colleagues used Twitter, along with other social media, to keep up-to-date with other colleagues and contacts for the trivia of life, the company and anything else they fancied. Both Giles and Kathy had become connected as 'followers' in this loop and he occasionally took a look at her avatar to see what was happening in her life, her family and the like.

The question of how to make the first relationship step confounded him. He did not want to make it awkward as 'the boss', although they were not directly working with each other, and simply didn't just want to say 'let's go for dinner', because he was aware of her time commitment to her family and stealing an evening away from her child could be thought of as a selfish start. This personal and emotional conundrum did not get off his 'to do' list for many weeks, reappearing almost permanently in his mind with annoying regularity.

His computer's inbox was barraged with its daily intake of all things advertising: problems and offers of lunch, which he endeavoured to decline at the busiest part of his year. On his return from an internal meeting, one entry drew his attention; it contained inspiring words from the London Summer Games and confirmation of his ticket order.

Giles was thrilled to have secured three tickets to the London Games, although this was slightly mixed with a tinge of disappointment because he had applied for ten in the ticket application process, and he tweeted the good news to his followers. As anticipated, he received the usual bravado led responses from the usual suspects, but also one from Kathy saying that she had tried to take Jess, but had failed in the system.

Giles, with little thought and his Twitter account flowing, direct messaged her in response to suggest a date at the Velodrome for the three of them. Having pressed send, he realised that this just might be the appropriate breakthrough excuse he had been looking for. Kathy accepted immediately, offering to pay her share.

Giles happily agreed to pay for the three glossy tickets, and as a happily negotiated concession, bowed to Kathy's request that she could buy lunch on the day for the trio once at the venue.

Never had fewer than 140 characters meant so much to Giles, and his faith in social media took a giant leap forward – along with Kathy, his Social Media Manager who sent the return tweet. His relief in securing a date was palpable, partly because he had achieved the first step, but also because it was done so simply, with a style he could have only dreamt of putting into one of his own adverts. How ironic.

Having paid for the three tickets, in one of the middle weekends of the Games, he marked it red in his computer diary and sent an invite to Kathy to secure the date; an acceptance was received promptly. The tickets arrived in the post after a few days and he placed them on his personal office cork board calendar, often glancing at them with excited bemusement at this achievement and the anticipation of the day itself.

Giles found the wait to the date a huge conflict in his mind. He wanted to shout from the rooftops that he had tickets to the Games and, more importantly, that he was going with Kathy, but then understood that keeping a low profile on these topics would be the best and most appropriate approach to take. Also, the novelty of having tickets soon wore off when many others in the office, and his varying social groups, declared their successful hands in going to varying venues to admire the best of the best compete for treasured accolades.

Work was as ever busy and the few weeks flew by until the Games. Many business related distractions were available for both Kathy and Giles to ensure that, reluctantly, office contact was kept to a minimum. The sealing of a new valuable contract in Washington kept Giles in America for the highly focused negotiations and, with the signed agreement now secure in his office, his time would free a little and his mind could now re-focus on people closer, hopefully, to his heart. Sure, he had a few breaks to see some sights whilst in the US and this had given him time to think about home: the cat being looked after by Mrs Cormack, his loyal cleaner, and, of course, Kathy, meeting her daughter and the day they would soon share. It was the highlight of the month to come and this could not help but lift his very soul at the prospect.

On his return, Giles was able to catch up with Kathy and gave her a call to say 'hi' and to check that all was set for the forthcoming Sunday – not wanting this longed for opportunity to go wrong. They chatted and Giles asked if Kathy or Jess needed anything when they arrived at his home. She was pleased to hear from him and they caught up a little about nothing in particular to do with his recent trip, work and life in general before confirming all the details, checking phone numbers and agreeing logistics accordingly.

The bright sunlight was welcomed by Giles on the Sunday morning, the day of their much anticipated trip east to the Games. The agreed rendezvous was 9.15 in the morning at his conveniently located two bedroom apartment. Duster meowed loudly at the door, welcoming them. Rubbing against them, the cat found these unexpected guests great fun and enjoyed them with great excitement. Jess, who had never had real contact with a cat before, was excited by the furry affection she received and was very attentive to his playful purring.

'Hi, hi, come in, come in!' Giles welcomed his visitors, beaming at them as they crossed the threshold of the apartment, reciprocal smiles on their faces.

'What's the cat called please?', asked Jess, not turning from the focus of her affection.

'Duster!', Giles positively responded, pleased that Jess seemed immediately at home. He reached over to help them both off with their coats, and showed them into his apartment.

'Good journey up?', he enquired of Kathy, gently leaning forward to welcome her with a kiss to her soft cheek. Her perfume filled his head with its intoxicating fragrance.

'Yes, great, so many people coming into town on the train for this today, it's really quite exciting!', she returned the affection at the same time. 'We had a great chat with lots of them, didn't we Jess?', asked Kathy of her daughter, who clearly wasn't listening to a word.

'Why Duster?', came the anticipated response, with a delighted voice, as Duster warmed to Jess's welcome, if not slightly heavy handed affection, nuzzling into the hand that fondled his chin.

'Because he's the only Duster I have!', Giles chuckled, knowing this was not true and also knowing that if Mrs Cormack heard him dismissing her work in this way, he would be in difficulty. He had been slightly untrue to himself when referring to things he had kept since his divorce, keeping Mrs Cormack was one bonus he often forgot.

Any typically childlike inhibitions faded almost immediately from Jess as she forgot herself in favour of the cat and the excitement of the day. She was dressed smartly, Giles had anticipated little else, in jeans, long-sleeve tee shirt and sturdy bright trainers. Her straight hair was tied back in a ponytail, and a small back pack over her light anorak was collected by Giles.

As he ushered them up the hallway, he admired Kathy as she entered the lounge. She too looked prepared for the day somewhat mirroring her daughter, but instead carried her attire with adult panache: make-up exact and tee shirt cut to a slightly provocative level, delightfully revealing of her gentle cleavage, crisp white bra cup edge defining her curves. Dark, heavy Jackie O style sun glasses nearly fell from their perch on the top of her groomed, silky hair as Kathy and Jess were both gently ushered into the lounge by Giles, and towards the view over the Thames.

Jess made her way to the mid-blue metal balcony and admired the magnificent view of Tower Bridge and its brightly coloured ringed Games adornment, and the soon to be complete glistening Shard tower behind. Giles and Kathy made sure that they had everything they needed for the day out. Duster seemed unamused by the exit of his new found friend and returned to the warmth of his favourite windowsill. Giles checked he had his mobile, keys and wallet and shot a furtive and slightly vain glance in the mirror to make sure he was looking his best, before closing the wood front door and catching up with the others who were holding the metal lift door open.

Jessica, Jess for short, was aged seven, well 'seven and half' as he was firmly corrected later in the day. She had long strawberry blonde hair, and many of her father's features, which included her love of chocolate. She was energetic, but average at school, and a bit of a day-dreamer, however, nothing too concerning. Newly addicted to the latest Angry Birds game on her mother's mobile phone, Jess was a happy-go-lucky child, however she had missed the stability of the family unit that had included her father before the divorce. Kathy's parents were relaxed in their manner and style and were very supportive of her in her career, filling in for Kathy by taking and collecting Jess from school and helping with homework. They were retired and now very much part of the fabric of this unit. Jess and her grandparents would need to be accepted if Giles were to commit to Kathy. It had come as a surprise to him that he was ready to take this jump, although with some fear of being hurt again.

They made the short walk around the corner to the Docklands Light Railway and caught the train from Tower Gateway to Poplar station. Jess skipped all the way and, at the station, managed to grab a single front seat to pretend to be the driver of the train. Kathy and Giles stood close by as the train rolled along, packed with travellers, destined for the same East London Park and its many activities. Police officers, Games Makers and ticket holders alike were all in buoyant spirits and the gentle jostling commute was a refreshing change because of its variance from the normal. At Poplar, they alighted, Jess was eager to scurry ahead, but was gently restrained by Kathy for fear of falling. The elevated platform allowed the summer breeze to refresh them before they headed towards Stratford – the crowd guiding the way in a herded stream.

There was some anticipation that the crowds would be large, as they had seen this building up on the train journey they had just taken. The nature of the growing throng was one of excitement, happiness and community. They made their way through the newly built shopping centre, the chatting crowd, children, parents, grandparents, friends and the like, all guided to the gateway and security cordons of the Games, most in high spirits as they talked and cheered, eagerly egged on by the Games Makers along the route who added their individual flair at each opportunity. Jess seemed very happy, both in the crowd and with her mother and Giles. Giles and Kathy easily exchanged light conversation – everything and nothing. Jess butted in occasionally to observe something new, and much eye contact where possible was exchanged with enquiring affection.

3. GOING FOR GOLD

Giles had never thought of himself as a dad, but the other spectators would not have known that their group were not together as a family. The Army team on hand for security checks clearly enjoyed the interactions with the crowd and once the three were through the gates, a walk ensued. They marvelled at the many varied venues for each diverse sport, mixed with the manicured meadows that kindly interspersed the landscaping. Neither of them had expected the beauty of the flower fields and this was a welcome sight to behold. The energetic crowds had now built significantly and sun burst through the light clouds. Kathy's maternal instinct to keep an eye on Jess was heightened. The changing views were spectacular and the suggestion to Jess by Giles of a ride on his shoulders was readily accepted by Jess and soon regretted by him as she bounced on his shoulders, pointing at every conceivable object she could see from these new heights. Kathy was delighted by his suggestion, partly because of the safe control mechanism it provided and partly because it was an accepting of Jess by Giles. She joined the pairing by inserting her arm in his, and tried to avoid Jess's flailing jean-covered legs where required, due to the ever building excitement.

They had made good time. The Velodrome was almost at the end of the park from the Stratford station entrance. They strolled past the media centre and the many TV crews and reporters plying their trade from the temporary metal cargo crates. In the context of other areas which had architectural beauty, these looked like an oversight, utilitarian units for global viewing purposes. After a long stroll taking in the sights of the park, the Velodrome finally came into view. It was a magnificent, wooden clad building perched on a hill.

With half an hour to spare before the gates to the Velodrome opened and an energetic walk now behind them, the waft of ground coffee and what smelt like cinnamon and baking enticed the three to the free standing food court. 'Marketing at its best', commented Giles to Kathy, who was now being dragged by Jess towards the waffle stand. 'Tell me about it!', she laughed as an order for three banana waffles with cream was made, whilst Jess located a suitable perch on the aligned wooden trestle tables.

The culinary delights were placed carefully on the tables for fear of the paper plates imploding. Although they did not look as appetising as the displays, they nevertheless lived up to the promise from the earlier sweet aroma. The warming sun began to become intermittent; shards of bright morning sunshine pierced the now growing and not unfamiliar summer storm clouds that appeared over the Aquatic centre in the near distance. Giles, Kathy and Jess were not concerned because their indulgent snack was complete and they made their way to the forming queue for their entry to the cycling event; no one was allowed to pass through security until the Velodrome was open. The queuing did not last long, and their tickets bleeped through the turnstiles, and they walked upwards towards the auditorium, with the yet to be used BMX track in full view as they passed.

Having made it to the cover of the Velodrome, a flash rain storm soon deluged the park as crowds scattered to all areas of cover. Their timing to the auditorium was not disappointing, as they watched from under the edge of the Velodrome the rain accumulated in puddles where they once stood, soaking others in the queue behind them.

They were held at the entrance to allow the temperature within the venue to be maintained and on entering the massive venue they saw its perfect, banked wooden track in all its splendour. The crowds thronged to their allotted seats, and the resident MC built the crowd fever with the encouragement of making it 'the noisiest venue on the park'. Enormous TV screens could be seen from each corner where minor celebrities were being interviewed which was then beamed around the world.

Purple clad, emblem-encrusted Games Makers smiled and helped flow the crowds to make it all happen, and the tempo lifted every soul that was touched by the experience. Jess waved frantically back at each Games Maker, confirming to both Kathy and Giles that this was her chosen task for the day.

The preliminary races of the respective cycle disciplines started within a short period of time. The crowd was hushed to a complete silence to hear the starting bleeps, and a roar was encouraged on lift off from the racers' holding stand. Giles, Kathy and Jess soon got into the swing of the crowd manipulation, enjoying the excitement of each race as the competition, tempo, heart rates and excitement reached new levels with each passing circuit. TV cameras panned the crowd, with targets usually going berserk on being spotted, thrilled at the exposure and the excitement of the building finals. Their control and personal boundaries relaxed and on the final race they found each other jumping for joy at a British champion; a new world record being achieved at the same time. Giles and Kathy hugged each other as they jumped up and down, both naturally embracing in the crescendo of the winning flag. The release was deliberately slow and their eyes danced in each other's as the embrace was completed; only to turn to see themselves on the big screen as a camera on the rail above them had decided to stop to use them as an example of what can happen when you get that excited. Kathy blushed, as she reached down to Jess, 'Look Jess, you're on TV!'. She pointed eagerly as the TV camera inevitably panned away from their position to observe other equally frantic crowd participants.

Once calm, if that was possible, they took their seats and Giles checked his phone to see his Twitter account light up with followers suggesting that he was a 'lucky sod' for being at the Velodrome to watch the cycling, along with additional comments of 'who's that you have your arms around?'. Some colleagues identified them immediately from the TV broadcast and Giles held the phone to Kathy, confirming, 'Well, we'll be the talk of the town tomorrow!', with a cheesy grin.

'Do you mind?', followed the quizzical but kind response, knowing they were all having a great time.

'No, not at all, it's great to be with you . . .', then looking down at Jess, who was still distracted by the cyclists in the middle of the track, ' . . . both', he added quickly.

Recovering his phone, he saw another direct message tweet had come in from his ex-wife, with her usual unwelcome sarcasm. 'Now moving on...finally!'. 'Bitch!', he whispered under his breath; the noise in the auditorium was far too loud for anyone to notice, and he decided that he would ignore such comment and do as suggested – move on.

With the cycling races completed, the venue was cleared and the three made their way out into the fresh air. The atmosphere was thick with vapour from the storm that had passed over during their adventure. With the obligatory visit to the souvenir shop completed, tee shirts purchased for all three, a great 'al-fresco' lunch in the flower park in the beaming sunshine was pursued. With cash pushed in his hand by Kathy, keeping her initial promise to pay for the meal, Giles reluctantly accepted and queued to get them all fish and chips from the faux 'Chippy', before returning to the flower garden and its relative tranquillity.

Many participants gathered about a pagoda, intently observing the notes attached to the inside of the shell that could be walked through. The three located readily available notepaper and pens and each wrote their experience of their games thoughts of the day and tagged them to the purpose-built wooden structure, next to a stream, designed for all to share.

Jess settled on her knees and scribbled away on the small sticky note with the supplied crayon, and wrote 'I want to be a cycle star'.

Kathy helped to place this in a small space amongst the thousands of others, adding her own addition readily, writing 'great place, great experience, great fun, interesting man'.

Giles scribbled away, admiring her note before adding his own, 'maybe again soon?' he wrote, knowing Kathy would read it. She did and pretended to ignore it; the curving of her lips gave the game away, and her spirit lifted with a glance to his eyes.

'Are we ready for home yet?', questioned Giles, realising that time had ticked on and the train to Kent would need to be caught from central London if all were going to get safely home that night. Many others also seemed to be heading for the exits too and he knew it would not be long before the turnstiles to leave would be heaving.

'Yes, good idea!', confirmed Kathy, reconfirming her agreement to him with a warm nod.

'Ok, ready Jess?'.

The scrunched disapproving face gave the answer, with an added 'huff'.

'Not even if I could lift you above all these people and carry you home on my shoulders?'. He knew that this was likely to work, as before, but probably at the cost of his spine the next day.

'Ready, ready!', came the childlike shriek, as hands and legs lifted from the floor almost at once to climb his frame to his shoulders.

'You are so going to regret this!', Kathy laughingly confirmed, beaming at them both and placing an exaggerated kiss on his shoulder to thank him.

'Hmm! I think you may well be right!', came the muffled reply as a foot swung past his face.

Kathy was delighted by the pair's interaction and with his potential audition as possible step-dad. She looked up at Jess to make sure she was secure, before collecting the newly purchased tee shirts and other incidentals and pointing the way to the exit. Jess continued to point at every detail and waved at every Games Maker she could.

The trip back to central London rushed by in a flash, as they were engaged in each other's company and that of the crowd. The big good humoured crowds enjoyed excited conversation on the train about whom they had seen and who had won. This made a huge change to the normal silence of the regular commute. After a cup of tea for the adults, and fruit squash for Jess back at the apartment and another play with the cat, Giles happily escorted them back to the train to Kent.

The great excitement of the day at the Games had not distracted Giles or Kathy from the real enjoyment of the informal and fun company they had shared that Sunday. The dynamic of their friendship had transformed completely, leaping from colleagues to something much more. They were both clearly delighted.

They shared a light, but nevertheless meaningful kiss goodbye at the station, neither wanting the excitement of the day to end, or the contact with each other that they had shared. Their eyes met as their lips brushed together. Jess watched intently and quietly, then blushing and giggling, interrupted the brief intensity. She had not seen her mum kiss a man since daddy had years ago, and then decided that she wanted a kiss goodbye as well. Giles, lifting her from the platform, gave Jess a gentle bear hug. She fondly returned the affection, and they parted, waving from the carriage and blowing imaginary and comedic kisses to each other as the trundling train exited the station, heading east and home.

He turned with a warm satisfaction in his heart, savouring the day's events as he headed for the station exit, his apartment and Duster.

4.   REFLECTION ON THE THAMES

His mind was in a great place on his return, freshened and uplifted by the day's enchanting company. Giles made himself a coffee and moved to relax on his balcony overlooking the lapping Thames; it was his favourite spot during the summer, since his move to his temporary accommodation. Mellow music wafted gently from his apartment's black Zeppelin sound system, as he gazed over the low tide of the Thames as it ebbed by, and realised that he thought he had found what he had been searching for. Love can happen again. His soul lifted with hope and he chuckled to himself at the thought and irony that he had been competing today: not on the track, but for the affections of Kathy. He was not disappointed with his performance.

For some time, he had known that he was ready to move his life on. He needed to share his life and knew he was a warm hearted, sharing man. This sharing was not going to be easy because he, like most people, wanted to share his future with someone special, someone he could really know, rely on, trust and would want to love him back, without condition.

Kathy's gaze on Giles was soon distanced by the departing train and she put Giles to the back of her mind, concentrating on her chattering daughter overflowing with tales of the day. Jess soon settled down in the warmth of the rocking carriage, and Kathy took just a few minutes of trundling train time to focus on the memories of the day and of Giles and their parting kiss. These mind wanderings did not last long, as her thoughts were interrupted by questions from her daughter. 'Can we come next year?' and, 'Do all cycle people have to ride on steep wood slopes?' and of course, 'Can we have a cat?'. Kathy smiled as she thought she might have one in mind . . . if its owner came too! Soon Jess settled further. With the school holidays in full swing, a day trip to Leeds Castle had been arranged by Kathy's parents as part of a group for the next day, and Kathy knew Jess would be buzzing from the excitement all week. The passenger crammed train took an hour and a taxi was hailed to return them both home. A quick reassuring call in the taxi from Kathy to her parents was made on leaving the station to confirm that they were home safely and that a great day had been had by all – Jess having to say goodnight at the same time.

Thankfully for Kathy, the bedtime ritual for Jess was achieved without any drama. Jess was tired and the welcome of her pillow and duvet were clear to Kathy. A kiss goodnight sealed her slumber as she gave her mother a big hug and closed her eyes tight.

Once asleep, Kathy settled herself downstairs on the patio in her small garden to enjoy the last of the sun; cigarette wafting its fumes into the dimming sky and a small glass of red wine perched on the garden table. Kathy knew what a great time she, let alone Jess, had had and satisfaction filled her being as she drew the last puff from her cigarette. Kathy checked her phone perched on the table and texted Giles to thank him, ending with a 'see you again soon x'.

From his balcony, Giles texted back with 'really enjoyed today, x', with many a similar feeling coursing through his veins. Giles pondered on the situation for a few minutes. He wanted her to call, just to say good night, just to hear her voice over the airwaves, just to confirm that for him it had also been very special. He resisted the temptation, although he was not sure why, observing some obtuse 'give her space' protocol that was pointless. He closed up the balcony and headed for bed. Duster clutched the windowsill still enjoying the last warmth. Giles, with mobile now placed by his bedside table, disrobed and prepared for bed, before lying naked on top of his duvet – the heat of the day still uncomfortable in the late evening. His mind was full of the spectacles of the day's events, both visual and emotional, as he drifted from consciousness. The vision of Kathy's beauty and kiss gently aroused him as he drifted away.

The weekly ritual of the 'how was your weekend' conference could be found around the coffee machine in the office kitchen on Monday morning. Most shared the glory of their barbeque endeavours or sporting champion's successes, and some of the office gossip revealed the presence of two of their co-workers at a cycle event on the Sunday courtesy of a YouTube clip which had been downloaded a few times. Giles smiled and confirmed that they were there, but diverted the conversation of any relationship talk to that of the spectacle of the Games. Most colleagues were happy to go with that line of conversation, because they either had or would attend the same arenas and wanted to share further the buzz that the Games had brought to London. Giles went to his desk with some relief that his wonderful day was at least not a secret any more.

The advertising agency was proving to be successful, although not without its moments, and a firm hand on the commerce tiller was required at all times. The business year's production project peaks were usually around the summer leading into the autumn and winter, advertising campaigns that needed to deliver profits. All knew this and much overtime was required during these periods to deliver, with some slack being provided in the winter months. Deadlines and project targets all needed to be tactically manoeuvred and Giles found his time was not his own. In years gone by this had not been an issue for him, especially over the last years of his divorce. This year, the pleasant conflict of wanting to share time with Kathy was a distraction. He needed to focus, but on the project in hand, and not the enchanting vision at the constant forefront of his mind. The pressure was telling.

To maintain his business composure, Giles endeavoured to keep his contact with Kathy to a minimum and, when they did finally get to talk, their conversation escalated into a heated debate about a project issue that had come up, with no compromise being reached, delaying the opportunity to meet up again. Giles tried not to make their argument obvious by closing his office door to keep prying ears from overhearing. They failed badly, and may as well have put a sign above their combined heads reading 'dating couple arguing here!'.

With the usual challenges of business, their shared frustration was palpable; both knew that they shared great affection for each other, but also knew that the situation was a little awkward. Kathy wanted to scream from the rooftop that she had had a great day with Giles and wanted to be with him again. Likewise, Giles just buzzed with his feelings for Kathy, but was unsure how to manifest these in the office environment they shared. Having had some time apart, did they feel the same about each other as they did when they said goodbye at the station? Was Giles running away from Kathy with the commitment of Jess in tow? Many men would, she thought, but she had thought Giles was different.

For his part, Giles was gutted that they had had a disagreement within such quick succession of a fantastic day together. How could he get the situation so wrong so quickly? He quizzed himself over and over again. The morning and afternoon drifted on, his sense of disappointment in himself only mounting. With the day at an end and still strapped to his desk, 7.30pm appeared on the clock hanging on the wall. His eyes turned to the space on his notice board that had housed the three tickets for the event he had enjoyed so much so recently. The space was empty, just as he felt.

It was a good junction to stop in the project process and he knew that the cat would need feeding. He thought about Kathy. He realised he had done little else all day, and guessed she would be home with Jess in Kent, probably finishing dinner and . . . He stopped, he was not going to guess, he was going to call to set the record straight and to confirm a few feelings.

Grabbing his mobile, he dialled her number and waited for an answer. After a few rings it went to her answerphone, her perfect voice melting him. 'Hi Kathy, its Giles, just wanted to say hi . . . and sorry about earlier. Hopefully catch up with you sometime. Say hi to Jess please, hope she enjoyed the castle', before running out of immediate things to say and hanging up with a humble, 'bye!'. He knew that he wanted to tell her everything, but not via answerphone.

His mind raced: did she know it was him, but decided not to answer? Was she ignoring him? Had he blown it? His phone rang almost immediately.

'Giles, it's Kathy, sorry, I was running the bath for Jess and missed your call. How are you?'.

'Hi, I'm fine', replied Giles, relieved at hearing her voice.

'I left you a message, just to say hi and I wanted to apologise about earlier, just a lot of things going wrong with the project and the last thing I wanted to do was to have an argument with you. Sorry!'.

'Hey, that's fine, I am really sorry too, especially after such a great day together'.

'How's Jess, good day at the castle?'.

'You remembered. Yes, she's great. I think she bored my parents rigid about our trip together. My parents want to know who Giles is, and do I like him?'.

'Ha! . . . and do you?', Giles added, not so subtly.

'Giles, I had a fabulous day with you, what's not to like?', she confirmed with affection and some reassurance.

'Thanks, I thought I had blown all of that out of the water earlier, sorry . . . again!', Giles floundered.

'It's fine, I'm sorry too . . . where are you?'.

'Just about to leave the office', he confirmed.

'Oh, you poor thing, are you OK?'.

'Fine . . . other than messing up with a beautiful lady earlier and hoping that I had done no damage and wanting to know when I can see her again, being unable to shake her from my mind, but of course not wanting to, I think the day went really averagely'. Giles confirmed the real reason for the call.

'Giles, I would love to see you again please, soon, if we can? And for reference, I feel the same if that's ok with you?'.

Giles sighed with relief, pleased his revelations had not spooked Kathy, 'Great! That's good news and I would love to see you soon please!', came Giles's almost childlike response.

'When?', Kathy asked.

Inevitably their respective diaries were busy for weekends, family outings, agreed socials and the like, even though their growing desire to spend as much time as possible together only continued to heighten, rather than wane. They were able to catch up occasionally on the phone, and an impromptu sandwich together on the South Bank was achieved one lunch time, Giles being sadly interrupted by a call from the office to answer an incoming problem from the States. Two weeks flew by before a text chirped on Giles's phone from Kathy suggesting a return match in Kent on a Sunday. He willingly accepted as recent opportunities to meet had been few and far between.

Kathy took the commute home by train from London Bridge to Ashford every day. This usually took just over an hour and gave her time to think about her day just gone, or to come, and she occasionally finished off a few emails on the way or checked over project data. It proved to be a reliable service and she had worked in London for all her adult life, meeting Matt, her first husband, there all those years ago. They settled in Kent over a decade ago for the convenience of being close to her family and this had worked well with her father collecting her in the family car most days from the station to drive her a couple of miles to the sleepy village of Mersham where they both lived, admittedly on either side of the village. The environment was clean and safe for Jess and the local pub was great for local gossip and local brews. The price of the train ticket and the travel to and from London seemed a small price to gain a good level of income and a good home location. Kathy and Jess had originally lived closer to Ashford, but the modest family home was sold to provide the division of equity required in the financial aspect of the divorce and she was pleased that she had managed to secure her turn of the century cottage so close to her parents.

From their perspective, Rachael and Jack, her parents, were only too willing to provide cover to their adored and slightly spoilt Jess, enjoying many summer afternoons after school with walks across the rolling Kent fields or running around to after-school events and helping with homework on a Sunday.

Both Giles and Kathy were keen to see each other, and tried to be relaxed about not rushing the growing and welcome relationship. Although the three had immediately bonded at the Games day out, they agreed to go for a meeting at a more neutral and calm venue: a wildlife sanctuary in Kent on a balmy Sunday afternoon and feed bread to the many and varied unidentified ducks.

Giles was collected from Ashford station and dropped off by 'Grumpy', Jess's name for her grandfather. Kathy's father, Jack, briefly said hello and welcome, and before disappearing, confirmed a collection time to take Giles back to Ashford station for his journey back to London.

The idyllic countryside setting was perfect for their outing together. The small lake was millpond smooth and there seemed to be a myriad of duck varieties, all scrambling for the baked offerings expertly thrown by Jess, along with the dark fish in the pond underneath the paddling feet, which disturbed the mud at the edges of the pool. The bond first initiated by Jess, Giles and Kathy did not waver and simply restarted from when it had paused, with new depth and energy. They enjoyed the local ice-cream and the warm summer sunshine, Jess taking to Giles with much attachment. She liked having a man around and hoped to get her bicycle fixed the next time he came, making the assumption that he must know how a cycle is fixed after all. Jess missed her father, but Kathy's ex-husband Matt had relocated from Ashford to South Hull and his two monthly access visits were getting fewer as their individual lives moved on, and through his other work and personal commitments. Matt had moved on emotionally from their division and had a new partner, preferring to exchange weekend visits for holiday time with Jess, if possible. Kathy had found this difficult, if not unacceptable at first, wanting Jess to see as much of her father as possible. With time, Kathy had become more relaxed with the access change, because the time he had with Jess offered greater quality and with it, love and emotional support for her daughter.

The afternoon and its activities flew by and the train times available for Giles's return soon began to tick by. Jack's car sat in the car park for an hour after the agreed time before they finally gathered themselves around it. The driver's window was wound down and the seat reclined, with Jack soundly asleep at the wheel under a shaded area; his muffled snoring audible from within five feet. Their laughing soon awoke him and he gathered himself together before packing them safely into the back of the car for the short trip to the station.

'Oh! Oh! Hello, hello! . . . sorry, I was asleep. What time is it?', said Jack, wiping his mouth for signs of any unexpected dribble.

'Late enough', smiled Kathy, a warm satisfied glow around her, her hand briefly holding Giles's before letting go.

'All ready to go? How were the ducks, Jess?'.

'Great, Grumpy! I saw the biggest one ever . . . it was black!'.

'Really, will you tell me all about it in the car? I think we need to get a young man home to the station'. Jack winked at Giles as they moved off. The trip to the train station was only five or so minutes and getting a word in edgeways with Jess in the car was fun, but a challenge.

The drop-off was swift, with Jack and Giles shaking hands, and a quick, 'Hope to see you again young man', offered by Jack. Before Giles made his exit, Kathy and Jess took a hand each and escorted him to his platform for the train home.

Kathy leant into his space, fondly kissing him goodbye, lingering for a moment on his lips, initially forgetting herself in front of Jess, and gave him a tight embrace at the same time. She was reminded of her daughter's presence by a giggle and a demand for a hug, which Giles was more than happy to oblige with. Lifting her to the sky, his fondness for Jess was growing in equal proportions to that of Kathy.

'Will I see you again soon . . . please', Jess demanded. Giles nodded and confirmed, 'Yep!', before placing her down safely.

'See you tomorrow', he whispered to Kathy, kissing her again on the cheek, as he rummaged around in his pocket for his ticket to join the open-door train carriage in front of him.

'Sure . . . see you again soon?', referring not just to an office encounter over coffee.

'Sure, try and stop me!', he smiled as he turned, stopping to add, 'See you soon tiger!' to Jess before staring down the train to find a suitable window seat. She grinned and waved, grabbing her mother's hand and pushing her body into hers for comfort.

Jess waved deliriously from the platform until he was out of view, blowing pretend kisses as she had seen others do before, a big smile on her face.

Giles knew he would miss them . . . he had already started!

Lovedon

5.   NO *WA*Y HOME

Their next meeting was sooner than they had planned or anticipated. The late summer heat had buckled the train lines again to Kent, and Kathy's service home to Kent was cancelled the next Tuesday night, with overnight repairs taking place and a packed bus service being offered as a poor substitute. This was thankfully an uncommon occurrence, but not unheard of, and the throng of fed up looking people queued around the corner. With many frustrated faces and mobiles wedged to ears, they confirmed her nightmares, as she came into view of London Bridge station, the Thames below her as she crossed the bridge. Her footsteps slowed as she realised the situation.

Her office had closed and everyone had dispersed in their varying directions home, or otherwise. The thought of trying to get home, let alone making it home, was daunting and unwelcome at the end of the day, having already left the office late to ensure the delivery of a media communication within a client project. Whilst walking to the station in the oppressive city heat, she skilfully pinned back her hair, achieved with an ebony grip which tangled slightly with her sunglasses, to allow the warm air to circulate around her slender neck line; her light, cotton, flower-pattern dress slightly sticking to her back with perspiration. She rummaged in her handbag for her mobile to call her parents to check that all was fine with Jess and that she was secure, knowing that they were unlikely to fail her, and confirmed she may be late, very late, due to the trains. Her demeanour was lifted as she thought of Giles somehow delivering her from this unwanted plight, and she texted him to see if he could help and if he was around. She now stood outside the station avoiding the melee of confused passengers also looking for alternatives. Giles, delighted by her misfortune and the unexpected opportunity it presented, called Kathy and willingly invited her over to the apartment, which was only a five minute walk. Kathy made her way there, hardly stopping at the station and tried not to make her acceptance of his hoped for invitation too obvious.

Giles prided himself on his culinary skills and was in jeans, T-shirt and cooking apron when she arrived, pasta already in the pan, and the Pinot Grigio out of the fridge was cool and sweating in the large glass from the heat of the summer evening. He had a quick scan of the apartment to ensure that there were no 'man' things lying around that might give away too much of his bachelor lifestyle away, although his previous hedonistic days were over and now only a memory exchanged for the sometimes enjoyable burden of running a business. His understanding cleaner, Mrs Cormack, who put up with him, had been the day before and, due to work pressures, he had not yet had the chance to wreck her handiwork.

Mrs Cormack was now firmly in her mid-sixties. She had an engrained but pleasant aura, greying short permed hair, and a smoking habit now very much curtailed due to cost. She went with the wage payer in the separation having cleaned in his old aspirational house in Clapham, before it was sold to pay everyone off.

His door entry buzzer buzzed over the sun bleached room and Giles sprang across the apartment to allow entry into the old converted warehouse building. 'Hi, come up, dinner's on!' suggested Giles without really checking who it was. Giles propped the front door open to welcome Kathy, who arrived at the apartment understandably perplexed and frustrated by the trains, but nevertheless delighted to see Giles. She stopped at the threshold and gave him a slow, lingering kiss. Giles held her in his arms and the moment lasted for a passionate few seconds before she was willingly ushered in. Having unloaded her briefcase and handbag, Kathy phoned home to check again with her parents that all was ok and to explain where she was and to check that Jess was secure with them. Kathy was quite matter-of-fact in asking if she could stay the night. Giles casually accepted knowing this was the obvious and hoped for outcome.

'Thank you!'. She gave him a kiss before texting her parents to confirm that she would be back tomorrow and a 'give Jess a kiss from me' from Giles.

'White or red wine?', Giles offered as he moved away, deciding that she may want a little privacy as he lifted her bags and took them to the lounge and placed them on the dining room chairs, before turning and heading for the kitchen.

'White please. This is really good of you, Giles', said Kathy, delighted that they were finally alone.

'Make yourself at home please, the balcony's open and the sunset is good at this time of day', he noted with a raised voice, assuming she was still in the hallway.

He felt her arms slip around his waist from behind; she had managed to enter the kitchen without him hearing, and he felt a fond squeeze before a slight release to allow him to turn around. She was exquisite and beautiful; Giles melted before her. Even through the heat and travel hassle she had just endured, she exuded feminine charm and sexuality. He placed the wine glasses he was preparing down on the worktop and cradled his hands around her cheeks as he lifted her lips to his. Her warm soft lips enveloped his as they shared the moment, tongues dancing with each other, passion beginning to rise in both of them.

The moment was intense and they controlled their feelings as he continued to hold her.

'Before I, we, get too carried away, can I get you dinner?', Giles beamed into her eyes, not wanting to break contact.

'That would be great, I am starving!', Kathy replied. Giles poured two glasses of wine and Kathy exited the kitchen to admire the view. Duster meowed from the windowsill to say hello, not wanting to miss out on any attention available.

Giles got to work on supper, proud that his bachelor cooking skills were being put to the test. Whilst in the kitchen, he smelt the waft of a cigarette secretly being smoked on the balcony as it mixed with the steam of the pasta.

'You know it will kill you!', he shouted with some amusement. Kathy hesitated, thinking that her discretion would allow her to get away with the crafty puff.

'Sorry, do you want me to put it out?'.

'No, that's fine . . . how's the wine?'.

'Good . . . thanks . . . very good . . . excellent in fact', the voice moved from its first direction.

Kathy gently breezed around the lounge, the setting sun glowing from the white walls and crisp lines of the warm, light-wood floor, as it kissed the large white rug. A glass dining table complemented the airy feel of his home, and she lifted her glass from its surface to investigate the paintings on the walls. Mainly numbered prints; some screen prints from 1920's Harold Lloyd comedy films. Their historic modernity reflected Giles's outgoing, upbeat nature, as did his music collection: CDs carefully stacked in alphabetical order on the fresh light-wood shelving, stark against the white walls. 'Quite in touch with your feminine side', Kathy suggested, as she fingered the plastic covers of the varying tracks. Giles emerged from the kitchen, two dinner plates in hand gesturing towards the dining table.

'Oh! Those, I like to think so. Mainly mine, but some left over from the ex. I'll pop something on!'. He leant to a remote control to let Norah Jones do her thing as background music and to turn the lights down. Kathy smiled, suggesting that opportunities like that to try and impress do not come along that often and were not that successful; she knew this one would be.

The steam from the freshly prepared sauce-covered tagliatelle rose from the white plates, its aroma tantalising the palate as additional cool wine was poured and they settled next to each other. The doors to the balcony were open to allow the now cooling evening air to compensate for the newly created heat of the kitchen.

The conversation whiled away the evening. They talked about ex-partners, how they met, what went right, why they loved and lost, why it broke down, how they recovered, why they recovered, how he really got his small Captain Caveman tattoo and its story. The delving into their pasts was mutual and sympathetic, and the trials of their work did not feature as they gladly investigated each other's worlds and the ways that these had manifested themselves and created the person before them.

Dinner was delicious. Giles was relieved to have excelled himself, with plates cleaned with torn shreds of the baguette acquired on the way home from the local deli. They left the dining table and lounge to watch the sun set through Tower Bridge. Kathy enjoyed an after dinner cigarette and texted Jess good night before they were really alone.

Relaxed, they stood together, arms leaning on the balcony watching the busy river-boats, plying their Thames party trade, go by – or 'river-boat scuffles' as they were affectionately referred to by Giles; drunken folk revelling the night away. The many speckled lights of London brightened with the fading daylight and the shimmering lights of the distant stadium they had only recently visited glowed to the east. The boat's wake caught the last blades of sunshine as its orange glow faded. Looking east, Kathy whispered, 'That was a good day out you know. Jess hasn't stopped talking about it . . . or you since'. Reminiscing about their Sunday Games day.

Giles leant to his side and kissed Kathy softly. The touch led them to stand and hold each other; their kiss entwining their mouths as their tongues searched across each other's, this time their hold not stopping as they enjoyed each other for a long, lingering time as their desires were heightened together.

He pulled back and looked at her closely, stroking her cheek gently before leading her by the hand through the apartment to the bedroom – the balcony doors left open. They paused at the bottom of the white, sheet-covered king-sized bed, his gaze firmly on her eyes as they kissed, sharing a heightened passion. His hand brushed across her breasts towards the buttons on the front of her dress, making ease of each fastener as his hands travelled down to her navel; her light, lacy, white camisole was revealed beneath. She tugged at his loose shirt and he allowed this to slip over his torso from above. Kathy's dress slipped to the wooden floor, as she carefully stepped out of it at the same time.

'I have wanted to be with you for so long', he whispered to her, placing a soft and light kiss on her face in different places in between each individual word.

'So have I', confirmed Kathy, her pulse rising with anticipation. They had both longed for their joining with great desire.

Kathy had so wanted the renewal of her sexual incarnation with Giles to be special, caring, loving and the situation she was enjoying met with her need to be loved. Almost clumsy at first, Kathy, who had not been in this situation with a man since her ex-husband, never feeling comfortable before, was very accepting, excited and willing for Giles to love her.

Beginning at his chest, brushing her lips past his nipple she placed kisses every few moments, varying the intensity of each. She ran her slight fingers through his hair as he pulled at his belt buckle and the zip of his jeans until they fell open. He nudged them to the edge of the bed and pulled his jeans clear, his arousal evident from beneath his tightening black shorts. Together they climbed on to the bed, their lips firmly secure on each other's as their tongues frantically explored each other's mouths. Each remaining garment had special attention applied to its removal, kissing each part of the body that was revealed, almost teasingly investigating each other's bodies: hers pert and cared for, with hair trimmed, his firm and toned.

He paused and reached over to his bedside table drawer, reaching in to reveal a packaged condom. She took this from him willingly and together they placed this on him; her hands rolled gently and skilfully down his shaft. Giles gently rolled his hand up and down her back as she completed her task. She moved and kissed his chest as her face gently pushed his body to the sheets. Her head moved to his and kissed him softly and intently. With her body on his, her legs gently rolled down the side of his thighs to the bed below. Giles positioned himself and offered himself to her. She accepted his advance, as she enveloped him as she glided to his torso. Their rhythm was gentle and nervous at first, physically enquiring of each other as they investigated this advance in their relationship. Her gold necklace rested on his throat as they concentrated on each other and their lovemaking. Kathy moaned as she enjoyed the physical contact she had desired of Giles and he tingled with the passion of their intimacy.

Their lovemaking continued and Giles rolled Kathy to the other side of the bed, not losing the contact of their entwined bodies, Kathy changing her hold by moving her legs over his, gripping his heated back tightly, needing him as his penetration became deeper in the process. She gripped him firmly and nuzzled his neck as their movements became progressively energetic, her breasts tightly squeezed against Giles's chest. Giles could feel her heart pounding as their combination continued, his firm thrusts being complemented by her returns.

Giles was gentle, caring, and respectful, understanding of her vulnerability, and enjoying her desire and the commitment she was making to him. He was aware of this fulfilment and was honoured that it was being bestowed on him.

The continued embrace built still further, reaching new heights of exertion before they climaxed together knowing that each had reached the peak of their encompassing and entwined embrace. Their eyes fixed on each other's as they both gazed into each other's souls. They shared the ultimate joining of beings; holding each other for some moments after their combined orgasms. Her body shuddered gently as his penetration peaked and after a few moments, waned softly.

Their grip lightened on each other and they slowly untwined. With a warm glow of mutual love and satisfaction on their faces they relaxed into the cotton sheets and rested side by side on his bed. Both lay speechless, almost panting for a few moments; both sharing a feeling of love and completeness that neither had enjoyed for many years.

Not much was said, not much needing to be said. Their inner most emotions were doing all the talking, and their eyes grew heavy with the intensity they had just shared. Both their initial slumbers were intermittent, trust of their joining becoming entwined in their physical attraction. Kathy found herself awake at one point simply staring at Giles, investigating his face with her eyes. From his furrowed brow to his hair all at the same time, whilst admiring his quiet, relaxed breathing. She felt relaxed with the love that they shared. Excitement for the future was diluted by the need to sleep and her heavy eyes soon closed as she drifted away on her pillow.

They were both experiencing a new level of love intensity for the first time. This enhanced emotion had not been shared with each other before, or any others for that matter, including their previous spouses. It answered their very dreams of fulfilled a life.

The heat of the London night was stifling and the white bed sheets were soon discarded because of the temperature, partly generated by their energetic engagement, but also by the warmth of the person they were lying next to, cradling their shape as they each drifted in and out of consciousness.

Although both were physically tired from the lovemaking they had just enjoyed, Giles woke briefly, his mind raced with strong emotions, satisfaction and love as they embraced and rested, entwined in each other's arms. Kathy slipped quickly into sleep. It had been a long day and a longer emotional evening and he admired her by the London night light that streamed in from both the window and the bedroom door – left slightly ajar from their earlier dinner. He watched her breathe slowly; her breasts pushed against his side as he gently brushed her cheek with the top of his middle finger. Her eye liner and mascara were heavy, but perfect in their application, and a glint of light reflected from her delicate earring. He had not spotted the simple gold stud piercing at the top of her ear before, usually hidden under her silky auburn hair, almost renegade in its uncovering to confirm a youthful arrogance was still being maintained. He smiled and sighed as the hormones in his body wafted him to sleep and he succumbed to the slumber that his mind now demanded.

As the night moved through its dark cloaking they both slept well, stirring occasionally and fondly accommodating each other as they shared the mattress and light, summer bed clothes. The cool of early morning saw uncovered limbs reach for additional protection from the chill. Both had shared long relationships before and were enjoying the renewed benefits of sharing body warmth; something both had forgotten. It felt so natural to both, as though it was always meant to have been.

Kathy stirred for a while before Giles's radio alarm clock burst into life and a 'Morning!' was whispered softly from under the sheets. With his eyes still closed, a gentle kiss was placed on his chest, her leg swung over his as she remained close to his naked body. It was so good to wake up in the arms of someone they desired and admired, having been entwined together for most of the night.

'Oh . . . hello in there'. Giles stirred and stretched his arms before placing them down on the curves of Kathy to hold her to him. Her breasts brushed across his side as she reached her head up to his to kiss him slowly, smiling and she lightly licked her lips before diving in to his mouth. Giles lay on his back and she slowly, almost stealthily, climbed above him; his arousal beginning to swell almost immediately at the thought of being consumed by his lover. Giles willingly wrapped his arms around her, excited by her renewed and enquiring energy.

The condoms were now long forgotten and with nothing said, their minds' ambitions alike, her legs again gently dropped to his sides. Penetration was achieved without delay, and this time they had a closer feel without protection and both tingled with this greater delicate contact. Their love making was less hurried this time, almost lazy in its ambience as they simply enjoyed the closeness they both craved. The close and uninterrupted firmness of her love massaged his girth bringing them both to orgasm within a few short minutes.

Kathy rested on him as his arousal waned. A smile came to both their faces as her head remained on his chest listening to his heart beat calm.

'Coffee?'.

'Yes please', replied Kathy, as Giles began shuffling himself from under her.

'Oh! Don't go!', she clutched at him, rubbing his legs with simple strokes; the proposition of further contact beguiling.

'I must, coffee, shower, work', came the slightly determined voice. The joy of her repelling this common sense was highly appealing, although he knew he did not have time to dwell.

'Well the first two sound good anyway', she said, as she lifted herself from him and headed for the bathroom; Giles admired her pert form as she did so.

Duster, the cat, looked bemused by this extra person in the apartment, having forgone his usual place on the bed during the night, displaced by this new naked being wandering his territory. Avoiding any offered stroke, he moved quickly behind the curtain to enjoy the warming morning sun, now glinting through the large windows.

Kathy dressed promptly and completed her make-up in the bathroom, a limited range of items stored in her hand bag, and returned to the lounge to check her texts and emails before giving a quick call to her parents to check on Jess. She agreed to leave work early to catch up on the family. Giles took longer to get organised, and Kathy left before Giles, preferring to go to work separately as they knew they were both growing closer quickly.

Entering the office, Giles caught a waft of Kathy's perfume on the return from the kitchen with his morning coffee. As they passed by they realised that the fragrance was from his shower gel. Kathy nodded to acknowledge him, trying to maintain what charade was left of their not-so-secret relationship, and started to move away – uncomfortable about the fact that she just wanted to jump on him. Giles understood this approach, but could not resist saying something with this opportunity; he edged forward to whisper that they smelt the same, their shared secret clear in his eyes. 'I wonder why?', came the sassy retort as she smiled and walked purposefully away from him and towards her desk.

He smiled and wandered back to his own desk, coffee spilling slightly as he placed the mug on the surface. Sitting at his desk he was uncomfortably aroused by the thought of Kathy, hoping that he had not just walked down the corridor saying 'hi' to his colleagues with a bulge in his trousers. The memories of his intoxicating night with Kathy were powerful, and the last few hours that flooded delightfully back were set to raise his blood pressure . . . and other parts of his body.

Lovedon

6.   BELONG TO SOMEONE

That day for Giles was manic. He knew his day was going to be busy anyway with his diary crammed full of meetings and conference calls, but one important project was doing everything it could to go wrong and the team leader in control was not overly helping the situation by asking Giles to stand in at the last minute. The day spilt over into the early evening and with most of the office gone, including Kathy, he made his way home to his flat empty, other than Duster, his feline companion. The bed clothes were strewn over the bedroom floor and Kathy's perfume was still on the pillows. The memory of the night before made him smile and he chatted to the cat about what was happening in his life, as he made some effort to tidy up. 'I thought you would have at least cleared up, Duster!', he said, assuming the cat could respond, along with, 'What have you been doing all day!'. He soon lost interest, and accepted the call of the glowing sun setting outside this balcony to enjoy its last warming rays before the dark was pierced by the lights of Tower Bridge; its augmentation of floodlit multi-coloured rings hung from its middle span, as he sipped a freshly poured beer from a tall schooner glass.

Giles thought about Kathy and nothing else, and his mind filled with the woman he shared his bed with the night before. Without planning, Giles texted Kathy to say 'Hope you're home safely and good night x'.

His phone bleeped with a response. 'No issues, home safely. Thank you for yesterday, missing you! X Jess says hi! X'. Giles beamed with satisfaction.

'Thinking of you right now, Xx', came his response, before putting his phone down to enjoy his evening.

Giles pondered what it would have been like to have met Kathy years earlier and to have been the one that she had married in the mid-nineties. He laughed to himself, realising that he would have been about nineteen when she was twenty-two. That was when Kathy was marrying for the first time, but it was a great era of emerging youth, political change, house music and renewed culture. He wondered if this was where the heavy eyeliner he appreciated and that renegade top lobe earing had originated from .His face relaxed into a satisfied grin, both at remembering those halcyon days of real freedom, university education sprinkled between raves, and of the thoughts of what Kathy would have been like all those years ago. His beer sank in unison with the sun and, having topped himself up, he relaxed still further into his chair and evening. Duster rested on his lap, not wanting to be disturbed when occasionally stroked.

The phone bleeped with a text. 'Think good thoughts, night X'.

Giles lay back in his chair, bare feet on the railings of his balcony and shut his eyes. He gradually drifted into sleep after his long day, and Duster took the opportunity to sleep as well. His day was over and with the temperature falling, he soon headed for bed after eventually closing up.

Having worked in London for many years, Kathy was only too aware of the challenges of commuting and the way issues, some small, some significant, can manifest themselves. Snow in the winter, flooding in the spring and heat in the summer. Her daily train service in general was very good; it was just when it went wrong that the process seemed to collapse at an alarming rate. The recent events in her renewed love life had changed her view on this subject, as it now provided an excuse to be with Giles when things went wrong. She found herself almost hoping that they would go wrong, not that as their relationship flourished they needed an excuse. It reminded her of her youth, but she was no longer eighteen and had other commitments, namely Jess. This travel disruption also brought with it the anxiety of being away from her beloved daughter, who was still so young, but growing up so fast: aged seven, but going on fifteen, it seemed at times. The love of Kathy's parents and their welcome involvement was of great comfort and all her family recognised that Kathy was ready to move on, based on accounts from all that Giles seemed to be a great guy for her to be with. They had commented as such about her recent change in persona and attitude, which they happily approved of. As Giles became a regular fixture, even Jess had not stopped mentioning him and the day she had in London . . . or the ducks in Kent.

The following week, the heat of the summer took its toll again on Kathy's routine and the evening rush hour train was delayed, but was at least announced early. It had been difficult to get into work that day, arriving fifty minutes late, and much to her annoyance she had to postpone her first project meeting of the day, scheduled for 9.15 am. Kathy did not hesitate, knowing her parents would be in control of Jess, and called Giles to ask if she could stay, not planning to even attempt to undertake the extended journey back to Kent. Giles did not miss the opportunity in agreeing. He had missed her since their last encounter, although, almost like a chastised child, he noted that he had not been food shopping and they would need to get something on the way home.

After the call, he paused for a moment to gather his rushing thoughts as to where he was in himself, his feelings roller coasting with joy, but with a fear of revealing his innermost being. The sex they had shared was simply mind-blowing; he felt that he had never experienced such a total immersion in someone's soul before. Even his younger exploits had not come close, and he could not remember sharing something so meaningful with his ex-wife. He began to realise that he was falling head-over-heels in love – somewhere he had not been for a long time. He chuckled at the thought, but this was soon followed by a humbling feeling that he had never relished before; a realisation that Kathy was what he wanted in his life, and with this change, a realisation that he had been missing this feeling from his life – for all of his life. He reflected on the magnitude of this beautiful revelation, satisfaction and completeness coursing through his very soul.

As the afternoon slipped on, Giles called back to suggest that as it was a warm and balmy evening, they could walk together down the Embankment to his home for dinner and a glass of wine. 'Lovely, great idea!', Kathy replied, with a 'got to go, another call coming in, catch you about six, bye!', before hanging up. Both looked forward to the romantic stroll planned. On leaving the building, he offered his arm and they grandly paraded towards the footpath, avoiding the occasional jogger and cyclist, as they meandered back to the apartment taking in the views and stopping for a drink at a local pub along the way. The local deli had a fresh baguette, olives and cheese, and a mini picnic was simply created as a feast for home.

Their love for each other was slowly, but surely, evolving on each encounter, each investigating and confirming subtle points about the personality that they clearly cherished before them. Giles did not want it to be about sex, or lust (although they were enjoying this renewed experience), but about being with someone, being part of a shared life, being loved. With dinner completed, washing up done together, tired eyes were comforted and rested. Their contact in their shared bed was mutually controlled, respectful, tired and they held each other through the night, as they experienced inner peace and the welcome thought of sanctuary again.

'Good night', whispered Giles, gently kissing Kathy's forehead nestled just below his mouth, sharing the same cushion.

'Night . . . I love you', came a quiet and tired response from Kathy; the resistance to letting each other know waning.

Giles kissed her head again, 'I love you', he whispered, trying to be calm about the best thing he had heard for years hoping that she would not feel his increased heartbeat.

He lay there for a while, Kathy in his arms, no longer wanting to be single and free, but wanting to belong to someone: to Kathy. He always had wanted this, but his previous choice had proved to be misguided – eventually.

Kathy drifted off to sleep in his arms, before rolling away to her own space, the summer heat penetrating the night atmosphere. Giles admired her shape under the shared white sheets through the night lights of London piercing the old metal framed windows: svelte and shaven legs exposed from the knee downwards, leading to small feet, toes manicured with red nail varnish, closely matching her lipstick. Her face looked at peace as she breathed gently, almost silently, with her hand resting on his thigh;

almost in an act of re-assurance that he was real, and not a fantastic dream that would vanish at the end of her slumber. He again found himself stroking her cheek, as he had done on the first night they had spent together. A glow from her berry coloured lips returned the memory to him. This was becoming a habit he didn't want to lose. He rested his hand in the dip of her waist, a surety to confirm that she was real and she was with him. He kept it there as his eyes closed and his mind wandered to places unknown.

The morning was brought to life with a start; Kathy jumped and took a sharp intake of breath muffling a squeal, as Duster lay at the bottom of the bed licking her toes. She looked around the room and down to see Duster staring back at her, his eyes bright, wide and aloof, as only a cat can do. She looked at the window and Giles beside her to remember where she was as she saw his large feet sticking out from the bed sheets. Her heart rested from its bold beating as she leant over to kiss Giles on his shoulder. 'Morning', she whispered. Giles stirred from the kiss and the commotion and she reassured him by kissing his chest before rising to leave the bedroom, clutching her shirt for some modesty, to check her phone and send a text to home, her parents and Jess. Giles caught a glimpse of her bare form as she left the bedroom and admired his view with a smile before closing his eyes, noting to the cat, 'She likes us, Duster!', with a wink and a Cheshire cat grin across his face.

Giles lay with his eyes closed, facing upwards. Kathy returned to the bedroom after a few minutes, her phone bleeping occasionally from the lounge with texts, to see that Giles had an erection under the white sheets. She admired his shape as she approached, joining him on the bed and sliding under the sheet they shared. She casually stroked his protrusion as her hand glided past, to rest her slim, light-skinned torso next to his – a warm glow from her expression. She stroked her painted finger nails across Giles's Captain Caveman tattoo, gently kissing it with a smile, before looking up and leaning in further to accept his morning advance, making her lips sing, her small pert breasts softly rubbing their nipples against his bed-warm chest.

Their mutual desire exploded as they gently ravished each other at first. Then it became torrid in their need to be joined, intoxicating and lustful this time with any inhibitions of the first encounters being dispelled. Ardour furthered, as the novelty of being loved again only increased, and their desire increased with their passion.

They began to reach an accord of conjoined rhythm, gyrating together in unison. Giles occasionally arched his back from above her slim frame, tilting his head down and to each side to gently kiss and suckle her small darkened nipples one by one. He received a heightened reaction with each switch he made before returning his enquiring lips to hers, urgently seeking her tongue with his. They rolled in the bed, not wanting to release their leg-entwined grip on their love making. His masculine hands rolled across the contours of her spine as they massaged their way down to the top of her smooth bottom – stopping just before, to sense the subtle dimples at the arch of her back. The messages from his fingers heightened his desire as they continued on their quest over her continuing curves. He held her closer to him, wanting his penetration to go softly deeper, wanting to be part of Kathy's very being and her of Giles; their combined ecstasy reached previously uncharted heights. The intensity of their combined love making was incredible to both, with exhaustion following soon behind as they reached the limits of their tolerances together; their juices avidly racing to mix with each other, both their bodies convulsing at their peak in harmony, a pattern both hoped could be repeated again and again.

They lay on the dishevelled bedclothes both facing the ceiling, both panted furiously at first, with the occasional large gulps of air being inhaled before they relaxed slowly. A glistening of sweat uniformly covered their faces as they lay, relishing the experience they had mutually shared and loved. Kathy's hand shuffled across to reach Giles's accepting hand, gripping entwined digits tightly, and they continued to lay with each other, eyes closing occasionally.

'What are you thinking?', whispered Giles after a minute or so.

'Wow!', came the soft reply, somehow perfectly summing up how they both felt. 'I could get used to this!'.

'Yes. Wow!', agreed Giles after a few seconds delay, before he rolled toward Kathy and kissed her softly on the cheek before closing his eyes again – more purposefully this time, as he snuggled up to her warm body. Kathy continued to stare into space for a few moments more, fulfilment bristling through her veins, her heart continuing to pound in her chest with their encompassing exploits, before she too succumbed to rest and her eyes closed. Their wafting rest was short-lived as time ticked by and the day's duties meant that the situation could not be held for long, but only designated to the forefront of their memory banks. They dressed for work, deliberately bumping into each other in the process to snatch kisses and embraces at every opportunity.

He made Kathy a cup of coffee as she dressed in her smart jacket and light slacks. She quickly admired the view from the balcony whilst having half a quick cigarette, the scent unavoidably wandering back into the room through the aroma of the coffee being prepared.

Giles brought the coffee through, black and strong, with half a teaspoon of sugar.

'Just as you like it!', he exclaimed, hoping that his now addled memory had not failed him. A prompt expulsion of cigarette smoke was squeezed from the side of her mouth, as she lifted the mug to her newly lipsticked lips.

'Perfect . . . thank you . . . you have been paying attention!', she smiled, knowing that he was keen on attention to detail. This suited her style and was a comfortable match.

'Yep, all the time, how can I resist?'. His eyes glowed at her, before a revealing frown broke on his face.

An awkward silence followed, Giles searched the ever growing Shard building in the distance with his eyes, looking for the right words to say.

'Listen, I meant what I said last night about loving you'. Kathy kissed him softly, reassuring him.
'I did hear you and I do love you'.
'I wanted to make a suggestion and don't know how to do this, but really want it to happen'.

The smile on Kathy's face dissipated, with unexpected and unwelcome concerns of a turn for the worse of their shared affection.

'I miss you a lot when you are not with me and hoped that we could arrange for you to come and stay a night a week, more if you want. Keep a few things here maybe, to start to be a bit more, well, 'couply', please?'.

Kathy put her coffee on the table, discarding her cigarette at the same time and put her arms around him before kissing him slowly, their investigating tongues gently caressing each other's.

'Yes please!', she confirmed, 'I would love that.' She leant forward and kissed him again, this time with more amorous and vigorous overtones. Her hand, now wrapped around his shirt-covered waist, moved slowly and deliberately down to his bottom, before provocatively squeezing it.

The delight on Giles's face was clear to see.

'Well that's me late to work; I hope you have an understanding boss!', he said, as he scooped her from the floor, kissing her madly with the occasional raspberry blown on any exposed skin. He led her back into the apartment, deliberately but clumsily aiming towards the bedroom; Kathy screamed and laughed at the excitement and anticipation.

The renewed arousal continued with the newly donned attire being snatched from each other as they only made it to the lounge. Giles put Kathy down to make sure he did not break anything, or anyone.

'You have a dirty laugh sometimes Mr Giles!', laughed Kathy, adding 'I know what you need, WASHING!'. She dragged him into the bathroom and into the shower.

The line of clothes across the lounge leading to the bathroom confirmed their failure to make it to the bedroom, and instead resumed their entwined, loving sex in the shower – water pouring all over them. The steam poured down the white tiles as they held each other tightly in a tight embrace, occasionally gasping for air from their exertion and the hot water that smothered their entwined bodies from above. The odd slip of feet required new positioning to be enjoyed, with Kathy eventually being hemmed to the warmed tiles; her glistening legs in a vice like grip around his lower buttocks and her arms over his shoulders holding him tightly as he gently rocked his pelvis with hers. The combination was a new diversity to their sexual understanding. He cradled her with his hands from beneath her, holding her petite form as his body paused as he reached his limit; Kathy welcomed his coursing orgasm. Breathless, she whispered in his ear, 'Got you first'. Kissing him and holding him tighter than before, she let out a gentle moan as her body followed suit; Giles felt the repeated tingle as her body bonded to his. They kissed passionately, water splashing over their faces, repeating their love messages to each other as though it was something they had never discovered before. The drying process of towelling each other down took them both some time, with investigations of intimate parts of each other's bodies being willingly and lovingly caressed, kissed and fondled at every opportunity – proudly being consumed by their love.

They tried to make it respectfully inconspicuous that they were arriving at the office together and very late. This proved to be revealing to their respective colleagues, something they had both hoped would not have been the case. They were both a little sheepish and the thought of adolescent ways to make the advert of their growing liaison less obvious had failed. There was some relief in this shortcoming because both wanted to share the excitement of their growing passion with anyone who would listen and knew that, as adults, they should approach this with dignity.

They moved to their respective desks within the blue-screened office. A brisk 'goodbye' was suggested before walking past colleagues who were already beavering away at their desks – coffees in place, phones ringing, and keyboards chattering as the day's business events soon overtook their focus.

7. RETURN MATCH

The comfort that they shared in their happily growing relationship was a revelation and inspiration to them both. They had moved miles towards each other from both an emotional and physical perspective and anticipated – and hoped – that this journey of pleasurable personal discovery would continue. Kathy, delighted with the developments in her life, also wanted to extend the range of their lives together, both as a couple and as a family.

'It's all well and good me staying with you, "Mr Bachelor-type", but I think it's about time you came to spend a night or two, maybe the *whole* weekend, out in the sticks with us 'country bumpkin' types please?', she declared in a very feminine, but jocular fashion, '. . . and anyway, Jess wants to see you again and I would like you to come and say hello to my folks properly, if you will'.

'Wow! The heavy stuff', Giles replied, trying hard to be serious and failing dismally. 'When, when, when?', came his childish response, a big slobbery kiss applied to Kathy's face at the same time.

'Be serious! Are you OK with that? I talk so much about you, people want to meet you'. She scowled inquisitively to ensure Giles was really cool with the suggestion and proposal.

'Yes, I'm good with that', came the calm reply, like a reprimanded adolescent. He knew that this was a big commitment for Kathy and his puerile approach may not have been as well placed as he had first envisaged.

'Good, because I have agreed with my parents to be around next weekend and you're coming!', came the retort. Giles was surprised, but made pleasurably confident by the immediacy of the plan.

Kathy owned a small, two-bedroom, end of terrace, turn-of-the-century house in a cul-de-sac, overlooking harvested arable fields and the Chunnel rail link; intermittently punching the air with the boom of its sleek trains. The village of Mersham was beautifully picturesque, if not a bit too close knit sometimes, with all the usual facilities complementing the location of her red brick, tile-hung cottage. The property was slightly run down, but nothing a lick of paint and a screwdriver could not sort out, thought Giles on arriving that weekend. Fresher air and so much space to explore; it was a stark reminder to Giles that there was an alternative to city life, something he remembered from his childhood.

A cheerful family inclusive day came and went, almost a surreal day for Giles, not having experienced a family day out for many years, if not decades. Giles was slightly apprehensive of meeting Kathy's parents, joking that it 'must be getting serious'. He wanted the relationship to work, which he knew it was, and remained un-phased by this introduction, which surprised and pleased him. A barbeque in her folks' garden at lunchtime was followed by a walk home and games in the garden with Jess, before Kathy disappeared into the kitchen to make dinner. The gastronomic feast was perfect, even if Kathy insisted it was not perfect, admitting that her cooking skills were average, or limited at best.

With the meal over, Jess politely asked to 'get down', and disappeared in front of the Saturday night family TV, her muted twitching confirmed that another round of Angry Birds was being completed on Kathy's phone at the same time. Before the running around of the day caught up with her, she was ushered to her ablutions and bed, with a kiss good night being demanded from both mum and Giles. The washing up was left for another time and they gladly retired to the lounge.

The red wine flowed freely, relaxing them both into their evening and into each other's arms. The soft sofa was welcoming, allowing limbs to be flung across its length. Lying together on the sofa, with the wine and ambience conducive to their loving embrace, their initially playful canoodling became more involved. A pause, almost a ceasefire of desire was agreed. With a quick parental check from the bottom of the stairs to check all was quiet with Jess, the lounge curtains were secured tightly. Kathy, neatly perched on the edge of the sofa, started to undress Giles. She kissed his body as she went, and paused to bite softly at one of his nipples, with him reciprocating without question. They felt like naughty school children. He willingly stood to have his trousers and boxers removed, while Kathy smoothly, but deliberately glided her tongue down his hardening shaft as her head moved with the motion. Giles, beside himself with arousal, did not wait to remove her bra and delicate lace patterned knickers.

Pushing her gently to the sofa base, her legs either side of his, he pulled her knickers to one side as he knelt between her legs, caressing her chest as he entered her. Their passion was deep and furious, Giles's penetration reached deep inside her as she writhed beneath him, moaning with pleasure at their completion. Her nails dug into his back as she reached to pull her body closer and closer to his; her hips adjusted to allow his length to search even deeper within her. They lost themselves within each other as their love making continued unabated. Moving to the length of the sofa, Kathy wrapped her legs around the tops of his legs. Their motions became faster and prolonged as the crescendo of orgasm clinched both of their bodies; releasing his love to her, she twitched with ecstasy below him, as her simultaneous orgasm multiplied. She felt faint at the new level of exertion she was experiencing, but did not want it to stop. Giles slowed his gyrations above her as his explosion continued on its exquisite path. Their clinch continued with Giles staying within her and

Kathy, breath laden, laying beneath him – eyes closed and gripping him tightly. She firmly clenched around his manhood for some time, before gently releasing her hold and that within. The involuntary moans of pleasure had not been kept to a minimum, and they listened for a minute to ensure that they had not woken Jess in the bedroom at the back of the house, the heavy, old, brick walls doing their best to muffle the sounds of their intense love making.

The experience of their fantastic and loving combination had become more intense and physical as their continued exploration of each other had reached uncharted waters, and locations. This did not help with noise levels and they had both giggled lightly when either let out some audible exertion, with the occasional 'shhh!' being whispered when required.

They rested on the sofa, its grip on their conjoined torsos increased by their activities, before climbing the stairs to bed – ensuring that no telling evidence was left behind. The crimson duvet of Kathy's bed offered a welcome and comforting embrace, as they held each other for the night.

The peaceful night turned to day and the morning was welcomed with bird song and other noises, which interrupted their half-awake gentle fumbling of each other's bodies as the opportunity of early morning relations seemed to be becoming a reality. Giles glimpsed the clock on the bedside table, peeping an eye out of the body warm duvet, to see its digital figures read 7.08 am. He groaned softly and closed the duvet over his face again.

'What was that?'.

'What was what?', Giles expired, partly muffled by the duvet covering their position, concentrating on what he was doing, and hoping to do.

'I think Jess is awake'.

'Ah, hmm . . . do you want me to stop?'. His early morning erection and its intentions being made very clear, as he rolled on top of her at the same time.

'Absolutely not!', she exclaimed, as she prepared for the closeness she now desired.

'Are you sure, I don't . . .', Giles's words were interrupted by the sound of light footsteps and the almost theatrical entrance of Jess as the door flew open, a pyjama clad grinning child rushing towards them.

'Are you having a pillow fight?', came the young voice as they felt a child's body climb on to Kathy's wooden bed from the bottom, crushing Kathy's foot in the process.

Their anticipated sexual encounter ended in a second as Kathy exaggerated her morning greeting with Jess as though nothing had been going on; although her understated panting gave the game away for any attentive observer, namely Giles.

'I'm hungry, Mummy!', beckoned Jess as she jumped on to the duvet covering them for a hug; from Kathy only at first before deciding to kick Giles for fun.

'Excuse me, madam!', came the response from Giles before grabbing her foot and blowing a raspberry on it. 'I'm hungry now, Mummy!', Jess reconfirmed, tugging at Kathy's arm with much vigour to come downstairs. Kathy leant for her dressing gown to give herself some modesty, Giles chuckling at this awkward process.

'Coffee and toast for me please!', came Giles's jokingly arrogant tones following them out.

'Hmm! We'll see. Jess can decide that!'. Kathy blew Giles a kiss before turning, flashing her bottom from the doorway at him as she was led by Jess downstairs. The sounds of kitchen utensils, kettles and toasters rattled from the kitchen below with the faint waft of toast coming up the stairs. Before long, feet could be heard ascending the stairs again, a tray of culinary goodies arriving at the doorway. Jess took her place in the centre of the bed to ensure maximum attention . . . and toast!

Jess wanted to play Angry Birds, but Kathy and Giles had other things on their mind and a relaxed breakfast of coffee and toast, orange juice for Jess, was consumed as a picnic on the bed, before dressing and going downstairs. A quick half cigarette for Kathy in the garden followed, before it was agreed that a walk through the village to say hello to her parents was in order, and then lunch at the pub.

Real life for all parties, from Giles, to Kathy, to Jess had to start again. All of them, including Kathy's parents knew it, wanted it, and needed it, to complete themselves. They all knew they had the right, willing 'people ingredients' to make their lives grow further.

Kathy had admired a transition in her daughter. A new and invigorated energy in Jess had been inspired, she believed, from the confidence that a caring man had brought to this gently forming family unit; moulded by the love they shared and wanted to share with the family.

The cool of the disappearing morning and its autumn mist cover was waning to a pleasant ambience, and tee shirts and shorts were worn by the three as they closed the house up and wandered gently through the track-type side roads of the village to the main, tree-lined green.

'Are you now my 'toy-boy' then?', Kathy asked Giles on starting their walk. He had never thought of the age variance and shrugged at its irrelevance, but smiled as a party-piece opener to future acquaintances.

Jess dashed across the newly mown grass on the green, in its last growth phase before the autumn took hold, the fragrance enhanced by the young feet disturbing the uncollected cuttings. The Royal Oak pub was waking for its busiest day of the week, enhanced by its hanging baskets in fading bloom. A road junction was negotiated and soon Kathy's parents' house, a detached modern style home, was in view and Jess made a bee-line to their glass front door. Jack and Rachael were at the door to greet them by the time they had caught up and a warm smile was interrupted by a hug: both for Kathy and one for Giles from Rachael. This was a welcome greeting, but a surprise. Giles hid this latter emotion as they went through the house to the small back garden – the smell of percolated coffee wafted from the ageing kitchen as they passed the open door. The Sunday broad-sheet papers were on the patio table and had been carefully filleted, dividing sections of interest between husband and wife. Giles grabbed the sport headlines where he politely could.

Fresh coffee and banter were shared by the group in the garden. Rachael fussed over getting the delivery of mid-morning drinks right, while Jess threw a brightly coloured plastic ball between herself and Jack, occasionally passing to Giles to throw back. The warmth of the sun was absorbed by all, as many complimentary comments were passed on Jack's arboreal handiwork. The Sunday papers were revisited and dissected further, before it was agreed that Kathy and Giles would head to the pub for a drink and lunch. Jack, Rachael and Jess would follow on, once they had worked over Jess's homework, an educational ritual they had observed over the last few years and re-invented from Kathy's childhood. Rachael was keen to give them some space and they were not in the mood to decline.

'Catch up with you in about an hour, love', Rachael kindly ordered, as she leant forward to give Kathy an approving hug, just hanging on for a second too long to confirm to all that she approved of her daughter's new beau. She looked warmly at her daughter as she released her hold. 'Hold on to this one!', she secretly whispered in her ear as she drew back, giving her a cheeky wink in the process.

'Uh, thanks, Mum!', came the cautious and somewhat embarrassed reply, as she turned with Giles and headed to the back door, taking Giles's hand on the way to guide him out.

'See you in a while', Giles added, 'we'll save you a seat, probably in the garden', he confirmed.

Rachael began to clear away the coffee mugs and Jack reached over for Jess's green satchel tucked under a bench seat.

As they walked away, they could both hear the '. . . So young lady, what do we need to cover today for school tomorrow?'.

Jess's voice soon followed with a 'do we have to?' and, 'do you like him then?', coming from the excited squeaky child's voice to the rear of the house.

'. . . Well I like him', Kathy joked once out of earshot. Her eyes wandered over the view, a teasing smile covering her face.

'Now, do you!' came the relaxed response from Giles, grinning like a cat that had got the cream, 'and would it help if you knew that he felt the same?', he offered happily, adding, ' . . . and that he loves you?'.

Kathy stopped and pulled him close, wrapping her arms tightly around his waist before confirming, 'Absolutely!'. Their lips searched each other's and they disappeared into each other's arms for a moment, the two entwined in a melee of love and admiration.

Honk! Honk! shrilled a car horn, interrupting their passionate embrace. Both realised that they had forgotten to move out of the middle of the small house-lined lane. 'Get a room!', came the brusque curse from the wound down window as one of the locals trundled past in their scratched people carrier, obviously late for some event, and scowling their displeasure as they exited the lane.

Having hopped out of the way somewhat startled, they laughed together, snatching another brief kiss, before carrying on their short walk; arms around each other's waists this time, with Giles's thumb tucked in the back pocket of Kathy's shorts.

As anticipated, the pub was bustling, serving its renowned Sunday lunches and on-site brewed beer to locals and visitors. They secured a suitable table in the shade of an apple tree in the garden, and consumed a couple of pints of the local ale and a ploughman's lunch before being joined by Kathy's parents and Jess, as agreed. The lazy afternoon soon drifted by; the ambient warmth of the day and the effects of the local brew slowed the tempo down, and a soporific few hours passed until it was time for Giles's train trip back to London from Ashford. Goodbyes to all were kept short by the realisation that his train would be missed if he did not get a move on, and Jack drove him to Ashford station, as before.

The goodbye to Kathy and a rather tearful Jess was far too brief for all of them; it seemed pointless that they were parting. Kathy held Giles, and struggled deliberately to release her grip on the man she loved. Jess hung on to his leg at the same time.

He painfully extracted himself from the best part of his new life and made for his train. Once settled in his seat, Giles snoozed the hour's train journey home to London, catching a nap brought on by a full stomach and the gentle rocking of the warmed carriage. He had intended to think about some business planning, catch up on some paperwork for an early Monday morning meeting in Earls Court, but the snooze was welcome.

He found himself pondering on his cat, Duster, hoping he was OK. Duster would also need feeding when he returned and he wondered, just for a short moment, if he and the cat would have a more fulfilled life in Kent.

8. I THOUGHT YOU *W*OULD NE*V*ER *A*SK

Kathy was pleased that Jess was being collected by Jess's father, Matt, for a weekend in Hull. They were good together and she wanted Jess to know that they both loved her very much, their parting not being a real issue. Kathy still trusted and loved Matt as the father of her child, for the care and love he still showed Jess, and wanted him to remain a central part of her life, the pressures of time allowing. She was keen to keep Matt in Jess's life and this infrequent offer of visitation time was always welcomed, even though she found its sometimes random nature irritating. They had shown a maturity in controlling the situation for the sake of Jess, and Kathy was grateful for this.

Kathy agreed to be at home one Friday afternoon in mid-September, clouds gathering with the threat of rain oppressing the air, to arrange the exchange. Matt was driving down from Hull in his company car to collect an excited Jess soon after school. The plan was that he would pop in for tea at the house, and to refresh himself, before collecting Jess and her things and whisking her back to the Humber; a journey of about four hours if all went well, and if Jess did not need a stop. Jess's return to Mersham was planned for 7 pm on the Sunday night to allow her to settle at home for the evening, before returning to school on the Monday.

Matt was a large, gentle man and Jess enjoyed the time they shared together. She looked forward to her time with him, usually with a full agenda to make the time disappear in a flash. Matt was on time and in a hurry to return.

'Mummy's got a new boyfriend called Giles, Daddy', blurted Jess as she hauled her tidy, red rucksack into the back of the car.

Matt was cool with this and smiled at Kathy as he turned to Jess, 'Really! And is he nice?'.

'Oh yes, he stays over and is great fun . . . but not like you Daddy, I love you more!', came the surety as she shuffled into her car seat.

'Giles took us to the pub and I had . . .', the car door was closed by Matt, not in spite, but in the desire to try and 'beat' the M25 motorway, and the conversation abruptly ended. Jess could still be seen behind the passenger window chatting away, almost as though she had not spotted that there was now glass between her and her intended audience, as she waved frantically at Kathy.

Matt looked purposeful, a long drive ahead, glanced at his watch, as he reached for a lightly filled overnight bag before returning to the driver's door.

'I am sure I will hear all about it on the way home! Its fine', he added promptly, before confirming 'See you on Sunday evening, any issues give me a call'.

'Thanks Matt, have a great time you two,' her raised voice noted as she waved back at Jess, blowing her a few kisses, and acknowledging Matt with a nod. The car moved away on its journey north and home.

Kathy had discussed the free weekend plan with Giles and arranged for him to try the commute 'home' to Kent the same night, expecting his arrival at around 7 pm. Jack, her father, agreed to taxi him from the train station. It would make a change to pick up his daughter's boyfriend, rather than his daughter. Duster was being fed and watered by kind Mrs Cormack again, and Giles relaxed with the vision of the village environment that was offered by the cottage and its owner over the forthcoming weekend.

Kathy felt released and excited by the freedom now in front of her, like a teenager secretly rendezvousing with a forbidden admirer, and she scooted into the house to clear up Jess's toys and trivia. She then tidied a little and made sure there was some wine in the fridge, along with some bread out of the freezer for next morning's tea and toast. Once achieved, a quick dash to the bathroom was in order to glam herself up a little, having noticed earlier in the week that her slightly greying roots were not as she would want.

Tight black jeans and strappy sandals accompanied her un-tucked fitted, patterned shirt that covered the recently purchased black, ornate, fitted camisole, deliberately revealing itself above her cleavage. A small gold necklace with a gold heart dangled across her chest as she dabbed perfume on her neck.

Giles was on time and arrived on the agreed train, greeting Jack with a handshake and updating each other informally about their worlds as he was chauffeured out to the village to the east of Ashford and Kathy's cottage on its perimeter. The rain had arrived and a tight embrace was welcomed as they headed out to have dinner at the pub, steak and ale pie for Giles, and salmon for Kathy. The ambience was enchanting, before they returned to her empty house to open the chilled wine from the fridge and to share her bed and the adventures it offered without disturbance or a limit on the noise they made together. His investigation of her camisole and its rather rapid removal instigated an evening of energetic and exhausting love making, which did not limit itself to her bedroom, as their freedom allowed them to investigate new positions in new rooms of the house, without care or interruption.

Sunday came and went in a flash and the afternoon appeared before they both knew it, mainly because they had not appeared from under the duvet until 11.00 am. That was only to get coffee before returning to the bedroom and carrying on where they had left off, excitedly rolling around the bed entwined in each other's bodies.

Midday arrived and went, and a panicked dash to the corner store for provisions and the Sunday paper was achieved before 1.00 pm, and before the shop closed for the afternoon. The usual essential consumables were placed in the fridge ready to feed Jess on her return. A tidy up of the evidence of their own 'adventures' in most of the rooms in the house was made to ensure a suitable and presentable environment was displayed to Jess, and Matt, if he popped in before heading back to Hull.

A car horn beeped from the road as Matt and Jess climbed out from his hatchback car. Jess ran up the path with her rucksack, juice drink in one hand and plastic wallet in the other, squeaking and breathless at the amount of information she wanted to impart to her Mum that instant. Giles stood in the doorway trying not to look awkward or awry, but failing, until Jess gave him a hug as she then took him inside to offload her luggage. He gave a single wave to Matt, who returned the gesture from the car, before disappearing indoors. Kathy walked down the path to the car to collect the other bag, but Matt this time decided not to get out of the car and interrupt the happy family scene, and instead wound down the window looking rather perplexed and anxious.

'Hi, you OK Matt?', Kathy enquired, reaching for the bag as Matt passed it through the window.

'Fine, I just need to get going, sorry! I could see the traffic building up and I'm worried I may be late home tonight', he retorted, looking at his watch.

'Sure you don't want to come and freshen up and say hello to Giles and goodbye to Jess? You know you are welcome', she added.

'No, Jess is full of the weekend so she won't notice. Maybe another time on the Giles part'.

'Sure, did you have a good time?'.

'Great, very good, she seems to be very happy and enjoying school. Wouldn't shut up about 'Giles this' and 'Giles that', he poked as a small barb. 'Listen, I want to take Jess on holiday to Belgium at half-term in October; we are going by ferry from Hull. I wanted to make up for the few weekends I have not seen her and it's to an adventure park. I have given her a pack with all the details for you to look at', confirmed Matt, knowing that Kathy liked to rubber stamp her approval on these trips before agreeing. 'Did you have any plans?', he asked, knowing that this would be unlikely, Kathy having always preferred Easter and summer holidays.

'I wondered what that pack was', before confirming 'No, nothing specific. I am sure it will be fine, but can I have a look through the pack and let you know please?'.

'Sure, but I need to book by Wednesday and I don't want to miss the ferry discount offer'. He smiled, with a hint of pleading mixed into the request.

'That's fine, thanks for looking after her'. She smiled fondly at Matt, before looking back at the house to see if Jess was coming out. Judging by the loud giggles and yelps she could hear from her daughter in the lounge that seemed unlikely, both knowing that Jess was easily distracted.

Matt started the car, and smiled at Kathy before offering his goodbye and drawing away from her house down the road. She raised her hand to say goodbye and moved back up the path, awaiting an intoxicated child full of energy and tales of adventure.

Giles and Jess were already spread across the lounge floor, attentive to the volume of exciting information she wanted to impart. With holiday pack open and brightly coloured contents strewn across the carpet, Jess was in charge of describing where she was going, what a ferry is like, what she was going to do and when it was all going to happen. Kathy admired the vision for a few seconds; her daughter never before having such confidence, and she pretended to look shocked as she was spotted and was beckoned to the floor to join in the excited expedition planning. She knew it was going to be hard to resist the trip for Jess, even though she had no reason or desire to do so.

Jess was clear in her determination to go, and Giles, whilst Jess was poring over a brochure, knelt up from the carpet and whispered in Kathy's ear, 'Come and live with me in London for the week?'. He released his shelled hand cupped to her ear with a wink, and blew a kiss on his return to the document-covered carpet. She again pretended to look slyly displeased at him, mimicking total abhorrence, before nodding eagerly and rejoining the melee before her.

'You will need to learn how to say hello and goodbye and please in Flemish Jess . . . or is it French? Oh! I don't know, I will have to look it up'. Kathy looked confused. 'It's French, mon amie!', Giles confirmed confidently.

'I'm not so sure, my loovver!', the pretend 'Franglais' going astray.

'Oui!', replied Giles, giggling with Jess, who watched intently at this new dialect, not understanding a word.

The remainder of the evening disappeared over tea. The tempo was slowed from the early holiday planning excitement to allow a smooth transition to bedtime for Jess. Giles waited to help put her to bed, his previously unrealised paternal instincts starting to evolve well.

He had planned to return to London that night, but on considering this further, and with a little welcome persuasion from Kathy, a bottle of wine was opened and a night together on the sofa ensued. They chatted about

Jess, their growing lives together and about what was special in their individual lives, before bed and the early train from Ashford to London in the morning.

Giles caught the earliest train he could, having booked a taxi from their shared sofa on the Sunday evening, to nip into his apartment to change and check on Duster, before dashing for the office and his plans for the day.

Kathy confirmed to Matt on the Monday that she was OK about the holiday for Jess, knowing that this would also give her the opportunity to live with Giles for a week, in London.

The romance that both Giles and Kathy, and in a different way, Jess, had experienced had been both whirlwind and dynamic. Giles did not believe in fate, but did realise that they had both been in a good place to move their individual lives on. This hindsight had not been apparent at the time of their first encounter, but something had stirred both their souls and actions. Kathy had been concerned that her emotions and the love that they now shared had moved too quickly, but could resolve this concern with the knowledge that their contact and interactions felt so right.

Sure, there were going to be issues ahead as their involvement immersed itself further in each other. There were the obvious concerns about their union going too fast. Jack, had taken Giles to one side at the pub in Mersham, whilst topping up their beers, to give him his protective father sermon. He explained that their lives were going well right now and not to get involved unless he wanted to really be involved. Giles appreciated this additional part of the family tapestry that he was clearly adopting. His determination was unwavering that Kathy was his real goal.

It was not only the competitors in the Velodrome who had been going for gold, it was now clear that they had both found gold in each other, only this was going to be good enough. In their respective ways, they had both accepted second best in the past and both had lost.

The real love making that they shared was a new experience for both. Kathy had not shared an orgasm with her partner for years, let alone one together in unison, and found the elixir of this new level of arousal a reassurance that Giles was someone worthy of sharing her innermost physical needs. Her renewed desire for education and learning in the art of sex was compelling, and she was surprised with herself on this exciting immersion.

Giles also felt a renewed and curiously energetic, yet cathartic, interest in their love making, experimenting in ways he had never before enjoyed, or come to that, been allowed to enjoy before. He was pleased that he had kept himself fit enough to get involved, because of some of the flexibility he had investigated as their relationship developed. The intimacy they shared was palpable and he savoured this.

Kathy felt a completeness, a renewed trusting of a man that she had been concerned she would never share again. Not because of her personality, but because of the natural layers of protection that she had enamelled to her exterior through unexpected hurt and failing love experienced through divorce. She had grown closer to Jess as a natural progression of this disappointment, moving the priority of her life from herself to her beloved daughter. Giles's love had rekindled her belief in her future as a complete woman, one that is respected, treasured and truly wanted.

The damp and cold of October soon blanketed Kent with threats of winter to come. The departure of Jess with Matt followed a scrambled look for her passport and a pack and repack of everything she could possibly need to ensure she had the best time ever. Kathy had packed a bag for the London return match starting on Sunday and had picked out the best of her casual evening wear to enjoy her evenings with Giles, and hopefully to share more of the love making that they had, as she thought, become rather good at.

Their magical week together flew by with Jess returning from her European holiday adventure on the Saturday. The love Giles and Kathy shared with each other by the Thames in that intervening carefree week was magical, confirming further their commitment to each other and their future. Only interrupted by a child scrawled postcard on the Thursday, Kathy leaving her contact details with Matt, they enjoyed this intimate seclusion with vigour, desire, and above all love.

Both Kathy and Giles returned to Kent by train after work on the Friday evening, with both eager for Jess to return on the Saturday afternoon. Kathy had missed Jess and was excited to see her again. They settled home together enjoying their last few hours, at least for now, as a couple in love; soon to change into a family in love, as their total freedom would be happily removed by the return of Jess. Matt soon arrived in his hatchback car in the afternoon, as agreed, and eagerly anticipated. Jess had been sleeping in the car and was a little drowsy as she left the car, stumbling as she did and rubbing her eyes, pushing her body into her mother's embracing arms, before wandering away to Giles to share a similar hug. Although tired, she was thrilled to see them and was overcome with emotion in saying goodbye to her father and hello to home.

Matt and Giles exchanged hellos with each other, shaking hands firmly in that typically macho way that men holding their ground do, quizzically checking if each other matched what they had expected. This engagement was soon diffused, with both offering some submission to each other and moving on to the process of disengagement to get Matt on his way for the journey back north to his home and his waiting partner.

Jess shed a few minor tears as the time to leave arrived and Giles gently picked her up and placed her on his shoulders, partly as a distraction which he knew usually worked, and partly for fun – giving her a tickle as she reached the new dizzy heights. She sat at a jaunty angle as she waved goodbye to the hatchback and her father's reciprocating arm hanging from its window. She still demanded this high spot for a few minutes after he had disappeared from view and, of course, asked if she could be carried into the house in her elevated position, with Kathy ensuring that she did not bump her head on the wood door frame.

They unpacked her washing from the two bags, with the washing machine pre-primed to cater for such a load. Matt had never been the best packer of suitcases and there seemed to be far more clothes than Jess was sent away with. An early dinner soon followed and the tales of her adventures wafted across the dining table, as though Giles was a permanent fixture, not thinking it unusual that he was there, at her home, and staying.

Tired eyes soon gave way to big child-like yawns and rubbing of eyes. Giles raised himself from the table, offered Jess an outstretched arm, and guided her to her room to change and brush her teeth before putting her to bed. Kathy joined them to give Jess a kiss. Jess smiled sweetly, before rolling over, embedding her head deep into her pillow, seemingly asleep, before they could clear away her day's clothing and retreat to the landing.

Kathy looked relieved, 'Thank you! That was sweet of you', indicating his attention to detail in the care he had shown Jess.

'Just pleased to help, she's a great kid', he confirmed softly, not wanting to undo the work that had just been so successful, and wake her.

'She was very comfortable with you', confirmed Kathy as her eyes indicated they should move downstairs, some of Jess's clothes in her arms to add to the washing pile. Giles felt satisfied with himself, slightly glowing with pride and achievement as he followed Kathy downstairs to the kitchen.

With the washing duties in hand, and the loaded washing machine humming in the background, they settled down to their Saturday evening: a glass of wine and some crisps in a bowl to quell any appetite, neither being overly hungry. They were both exhausted, not by any physical exertion, but by their thoughts of the family coming together, which seemed to now be complete with the three of them safely under one roof. The usual evening TV viewing was as rubbish as ever and left on in the background as they whiled the evening away with discussions about Jess, Matt, his journey home, their own feelings and the plans for the Sunday ahead and maybe plans for later in the week.

With sleep catching up on them fast, they also decided to retire early to the warmth of the bedroom and the duvet. The autumn chill of the October night soon crept up in the older house, and Giles commented that he would fix the insulation when he next stayed. A quick check on Jess was achieved without disturbance before they wrestled each other to a comfortable position in the middle of the bed, a long and passionate, somehow assured, kiss exchanged, before Kathy drifted into slumber. Giles soon followed suit as the body warmth of their combined beings enveloped them.

They all rested without a sound. Only a neighbour broke Giles's deep and complete sleep with the disposal of his empty wine bottles being recycled, breaking the spell of the chilly morning light. His jolt disturbed Kathy and they both lay there for a few moments to let the day descend on their minds. Giles kissed her forehead softly as she lay next to him, distant church bells ringing across the early morning still of the village and fields. She returned the compliment; her gentle lips caressing his, as he repeated his affection, before she pulled her face away and turned her head on the pillow, facing his face, and looked purposeful.

He smiled, looking into her eyes and admired her slightly dishevelled hair, which she duly brushed from her face to give herself a clear view of Giles, searching his expression as she shuffled slightly in the bed.

'Giles?'.

'Yes, gorgeous', he responded, adding, 'what time is it?'.

'8 am'.

She reasserted her tone, 'Giles, I love you; do you know that?', she asked, both already knowing the answer.

'Yes, very much and I love you too!', he smiled, confirming his commitment by kissing her hand situated on his pillow.

'I have loved being with you all this week, and these few months. It has been very special and times I will always remember'.The intensity of her tone deepened. 'And I don't want what we have shared to end . . . '. Kathy looked him in the eyes as her face drew close to his lips, '. . . please!'. 'Will you come and live with Jess and me please?', she asked softly, searching his emotions for confirmation, before he replied.

'I thought you would never ask!'.

ABOUT THE AUTHOR

MARION CRICK

Marion has now been writing for quite a few years and hopefully you have caught up with her first few books, the Lovedon series as an example. If you have already read these, don't worry; Marion still thinks there is another twist in this tale and has penned a few thoughts as she wrote this latest book.

In terms of her background, the close knit community she shared with her parents and sibling were kind to her as she grew up, before finally taking the leap to administration duties in London when her experience of the daily commuter grind began. The after-work social scene was worth the hassle, let alone the elevated salary that came with it, enjoying many adventures in love before settling down, although there was not to be a 'happy ever after' just yet.

Separation, divorce, grieving and re-engagement into the social scene and into dating have all been part of the kaleidoscope she calls her life. This second round of coupling reminded her a little of those first few years in London, when she began to discover herself and her physical and emotional needs.

Can you reach middle age? Is there such a thing these days, and if so, how can you define this? Marion's middle age has not hampered her exploration of re-ignited love, sex and real companionship. Marion always maintained a diary, on and off. She extended this to a daily update after her initial separation, partly of the day's events, good and bad, but also of her inner feelings and the reaction of her friends and family as they evolved, and as her new love and desire exploded.

Marion's diaries have many other revelations within them and *Lovedon* is only part of her story and the stories yet to be written.